Praise for Beth Vrabel's Pack of Dorks

* "Lucy's perfectly feisty narration, emotionally resonant situations, and the importance of the topic all elevate this effort well above the pack."

—*Kirkus Reviews*, starred review

"Lucy's growth and smart, funny observations entertain and empower in Vrabel's debut, a story about the benefits of embracing one's true self and treating others with respect."

—*Publishers Weekly*

"Vrabel displays a canny understanding of middle-school vulnerability."

—*Booklist*

"Lucy's confident first-person narration keeps pages turning as she transitions from totally popular to complete dorkdom in the space of one quick kiss. . . . Humorous and honest."

—*VOYA*

"A fresh look at what it means to embrace what makes you and the ones you love different. . . . *Pack of Dorks* is the pack I want to join."

—Amanda Flower, author of Agatha Award nominee *Andi Unexpected*

"You won't want to stop reading about Lucy and her pack . . . a heartwarming story to which everyone can relate."

—Elizabeth Atkinson, author of *I, Emma Freke*

"A book about all kinds of differences, with all kinds of heart. Lucy and her pack of dorks are hilarious and lovable."

—Kristen Chandler, author of *Wolves, Boys, and Other Things That Might Kill Me*

"A powerful story of friendship and hardship. Vrabel's debut novel speaks to those struggling for acceptance and inspires them to look within themselves for the strength and courage to battle real-life issues."

—Buffy Andrews, author of *The Lion Awakens* and *Freaky Frank*

"Beth Vrabel weaves an authentic, emotional journey that makes her a standout among debut authors."

—Kerry O'Malley Cerra, author of *Just a Drop of Water*

Praise for Beth Vrabel's Camp Dork

"Vrabel has a rare talent for expressing the tenderness, frustration, awkwardness, confusion, and fun of growing up. VERDICT: In Vrabel's capable hands, the ups and downs of adolescence shine through with authenticity and humor."

—*School Library Journal*

"With good humor, Vrabel explores the pitfalls of emerging preteenhood. This quick read nonetheless effectively delves into interpersonal pitfalls that will be familiar to most older grade schoolers, and Lucy's developing insight may even provide a few hints for staying on the right path. Honest, funny, and entertaining."

—*Kirkus Reviews*

pack of dorks
SUPER DORKS

Also by Beth Vrabel

Pack of Dorks
Camp Dork

A Blind Guide to Stinkville
A Blind Guide to Normal
Caleb and Kit
Bringing Me Back

pack of dorks

SUPER DORKS

BETH VRABEL

SKY PONY PRESS
NEW YORK

First Edition

This is a work of fiction. Names, characters, places, and incidents are from the author's imagination and used fictitiously.

Sky Pony Press books may be purchased in bulk at special discounts for sales promotion, corporate gifts, fund-raising, or educational purposes. Special editions can also be created to specifications. For details, contact the Special Sales Department, Sky Pony Press, 307 West 36th Street, 11th Floor, New York, NY 10018 or info@skyhorsepublishing.com.

Sky Pony® is a registered trademark of Skyhorse Publishing, Inc.®, a Delaware corporation.

www.skyponypress.com

10 9 8 7 6 5 4 3 2 1

Library of Congress Cataloging-in-Publication Data is available on file.

Cover design by Brian Peterson

Print ISBN: 978-1-5107-3144-8
Ebook ISBN: 978-1-5107-3146-2

Printed in the United States of America

For Ben

Chapter One

This was going to be the worst year of my life.

I crumpled my fifth-grade schedule and the letter from my new teacher in my fist and blinked away the stinging in my eyes. Not a single friend in my homeroom.

Of course, that sounded less dramatic when you figure I only had four friends. Sam, April, Sheldon, Amanda, and I perched on the top of the monkey bars with our legs swinging down below us. Together, we were a pack, ready to take on bullies and frenemies.

I had once been one of the "cool" kids. I shuddered thinking about those dark, pack-less days that I spent fake laughing at jerkface Tom's bad jokes and whispering mean things about other people to my only-when-I-was-popular best friend Becky. But then Tom said he hated me, which made Becky stop being my friend at school, and suddenly I had become a solo eater in the cafeteria. And in life.

Luckily, Sam and I were paired to work on a project about wolves. We realized we were like the scapegoats—the wolves that all the other wolves in the pack loved to pick on. And we decided to stop being in packs like that and make a new one of our own, even though jerkface Tom called it a Pack of Dorks.

Sheldon, with his dinosaur obsession, and April, who had once suffered from a nose-picking addiction, also had been solo eaters in the cafeteria. Amanda had eaten with whoever she wanted to but only because most kids were afraid of her potential to slap off their faces if she got too mad. (It had never actually happened, but we all knew it was possible.) Once Sam and I formed our pack, the three of them joined in, too. And together, we laughed when people (ahem, ahem, Tom) called us names. Soon the name-calling just sort of stopped. Or maybe we just stopped noticing. Either way, we're better together.

Or at least, we *would be* better together. I shook the schedule in my fist.

This year, April had enrolled in a magnet school in

the city. Sam and Sheldon each had Mr. Grayson, known for his love of argyle socks and yoga. Amanda had Mrs. Mason, who had an unnatural affection for sunflowers and bumblebees. (Seriously. Her walls were decorated with sunflower posters. She signed her teacher letter with a little bumblebee over the *n*.)

I tried to picture Amanda, whose natural state of anger was just barely contained with daily meditation, surrounded by all that happy décor. I think she was also picturing that, because her face turned a little green. "Bumblebees make me angry!" she grumbled. Sheldon patted her back.

As for me? I was stuck with the newbie teacher who no one knew anything about and who probably didn't know anything. Miss Parker. Puke. Her letter was on plain white paper with typewriting font. *Boring.*

"Want to ride bikes to school tomorrow?" Sheldon asked Amanda.

"I can't. Someone stole my bike last week." She cracked her knuckles. "Dad said I shouldn't have left it in the front yard, but if I catch the guy who nabbed it—"

"A lot of people are looking for that guy," Sam said. "Mom told me last night that about a dozen bikes have been stolen from front yards in the last month."

No one said anything for a moment while Amanda muttered *kumbaya* under her breath and cracked each finger, her wrist, and then her neck. The *kumbaya* is supposed to be like a mantra that helps her calm down when she gets really angry. It doesn't always work.

Sheldon scooted to the edge of the monkey bars, preparing to jump down. "Mr. Grayson's letter has something in it about the election for the fifth-grade student government."

Sheldon seemed super focused on the ground. *Just jump already,* I thought.

He continued, "Applications are due by the end of the first week, and since school starts on a Wednesday, that's only three days to figure out if we want to run for office."

"The first week?" April echoed. "That's kind of crazy."

Amanda shrugged. "Well, the guidance counselor *did* tell us all about it on the last day of fourth grade."

"They did?" Sam and I said at the same time.

April laughed. "Yeah, right after you guys gave your wolf speech to the class. Lucy, you were too busy offering to sign people's notebooks and Sam, you were . . ."

"Trying to breathe normally again," he finished for

her. When he wasn't doing gymnastics, Sam hated being the center of attention. I'm not sure what that's like.

"Anyway, our teacher letters say something about it," Sheldon added. Mr. Grayson's letter was folded into a neat square and tucked into his back pocket.

I smoothed mine out again on my lap. Sure enough, toward the end, Miss Parker's letter said:

Calling all fifth-grade superheroes! Turn in your applications for student government elections by the end of our first week.

I snorted. "Like any of us stand a shot."

Sheldon, his ears flaming red, finally made the jump. Amanda slipped off the monkey bars on her stomach after him and they made their ways to the swings.

"Ugh," I groaned. "This year is going to be terrible. I'm going to be all alone all the time."

Sam bumped me with his shoulder. "There's still recess," he reminded me. "And lunch."

"And after school! We're going to meet in the park, right?" April chewed her lip, her eyes wide.

I nodded and made my mouth stretch into a smile for her. While I was worried about not being with any of my friends, April wasn't going to have *anyone* she knew at school. If April could do that, I could survive on just seeing the rest of the Pack at recess and lunch.

"Are you nervous?" I asked her as Sam jumped down from the monkey bars.

April nodded but smiled hugely at me. "And excited!" she chirped. When she got excited, everything April said came out in bursts. She used to speak like that all the time, but it was just one of many things April had been changing lately.

The funny thing is, no one other than our pack noticed. The rest of the school—especially head jerkfaces Tom and Henry—still said "ew!" whenever April passed out papers, even though she never picked her nose anymore. They still made a point to choose her last for sports even though she kicked their butts at basketball and was soon going to be a black belt in tae kwon do. Over the summer, her hair went from frizzy fluff to shiny reddish-brown waves and she grew about two inches. April looked like one of the models in the *American Girl* catalog, but she'd always be a nobody at Autumn Grove Intermediate School.

Once a dork, always a dork.

That's why she was switching schools, so she could change things about herself. Well, that wasn't right, exactly. She didn't want to change, she just wanted other people to see the real her. At summer camp a couple weeks earlier, April had pointed out to me that other campers—the ones who didn't go to school with us—had liked her, even looked up to her, thought she was pretty and called her popular.

I guess I could understand that. Here, I'd always be the girl who split her sausage skirt while screaming like a lunatic. (Warning: Lost and Found boxes aren't known for their solid fashion options. So if, say, some-one—ahem, egg-breath Henry—tips your lunch tray of delicious refried beans onto your clothes, you might be forced to change into a too-tight Lost and Found skirt. And if later, another someone—ahem, jerkface Tom—laughs about hanging your best friend by his underpants in the bathroom, you might forget you're not wearing your comfy clothes and jump to your feet, splitting your skirt right up the bum.) And Sam would always be said kid who got hung by his underpants in the bathroom. Sheldon would never stop being a skinny twerp obsessed with dinosaurs. Amanda would never stop being an angry brute.

The thing was, the rest of us were kind of okay with that. We had one another, and we knew who we really were and what made us such great friends. But April wanted something more.

"You'll be okay," I told her. "I know it."

April's smile somehow stretched even further. "You will be, too, Lucy. You always are."

Across the park, I saw a mom pushing a stroller with a baby inside, twin toddlers trailing behind her. The mom sat down on a bench on the opposite end of the park and opened a book, rocking the stroller back and forth with her foot. The two toddlers squealed and chased each other around the sliding board. Man, it must really stink having to have your parents hover over you all the time. I remember those days. Seemed like just a week ago that Mom agreed I could go with the pack to the park without parental supervision. (Okay. Fine. It *was* a week ago. And she texted me three times since we got here today.)

While April and I kept talking, the rest of the pack made their way around the park.

Sam was behind the toddler twins, walking the wooden boards that edged the park like it was a balance beam. Boys don't do the balance beam in gymnastics, but if they did, he'd be awesome at that. Sam was killer at the rings and the pommel horse. But he could've kicked butt at any sport he picked up. Like he could read my thoughts, Sam did a no-hands somersault along the board and landed perfectly. I held up my hands to give him a perfect ten and he grinned.

I'm still waiting to find my awesome—you know, the thing I'm particularly fantastic at doing or achieving. I tried scouting for it when we were at Camp Paleo this summer, and while I wasn't able to zero in on what I'm awesome at, I was able to knock a few potentials off the list. Such as archery (almost shot the camp director), juggling (accidentally responsible for April's concussion from a grapefruit), cooking (caused an "egg" and hot chocolate fire), and matchmaking (Cupid and I are not friends). *Maybe this will be the year of my awesome*, I thought as Sam meandered the edge of the playground.

Sheldon and Amanda were on the swings, pumping their legs and jumping off when they got higher than I would've dared. "Booyah!" Amanda yelled as she landed on her feet. Sheldon wasn't so lucky. He landed on his side with a thud. Amanda chuckled and held out a hand to hoist him up.

Sheldon smiled as they held onto each other's hands a little longer than needed.

"Looks like Shemanda is still going strong," April whispered into my ear.

I hid my laugh behind my hand. Sheldon, with his thick burst of black hair, skinny narrow face, and ironed-on dino patch sweatshirt, didn't look like he'd be a good match for Amanda, who towered at least three inches higher than Sheldon and only wore all-black mesh sports shorts and T-shirts. But somehow they were adorkable together.

I scanned the playground for Sam. He wasn't on the makeshift beam. The mom saw me looking and suddenly half stood from her seat on the bench, looking around, too. I couldn't see the little kids anymore either.

"Have you seen—"

My words were slashed by a shriek, the squeal of slamming brakes, a cracking thud, and a tremendous pounding that I only later realized was my heart. "Sam!" I screamed so loudly my throat clenched shut at the end.

April and I jumped down from the bars and tore off in the direction of the noise, toward the edge of the playground at the parking lot, just behind the mom. Sheldon and Amanda were on our heels. I thought I still was screaming, but it was the mom wailing.

As we got to the parking lot, I slowed down even though everyone else sprinted faster—my knees twisted and shook and refused to hold up my legs. Because there, between a car with a wheel up on a cement parking lot divider and the crying, scratched-up toddlers, was my best friend, crumpled up like a hamburger wrapper and not moving. "Sam!" I screamed, but it only came out as a whisper.

The mom fell to her knees in front of the sobbing toddlers, her hands raking over them for injuries. April rushed forward to Sam, her hand slowly moving to his shoulder, about to turn him toward us. Sheldon and Amanda huddled over Sheldon's cell phone. He was shaking too hard to punch the buttons, so Amanda did instead. "Yes!" I heard him squeak. "We need an ambulance at Autumn Grove Park. My friend! He was hit by a car!"

Slowly, slowly, slowly, April's hand reached Sam. He rolled onto his back, blood dripping down his face from a gash on his forehead. He cradled his left arm, which looked all wrong. A big shoulder-sized lump wasn't at his shoulder at all, but where his bicep should be. Another weird lump stuck out of his elbow. His mouth hung open and his eyes stayed shut. A soft, horrible moan leaked out from his lips.

Then, at last, my knees let me move again. I stumbled forward, falling next to him. "You're okay, Sam," I told him, holding the edge of my T-shirt against the cut on his forehead. "You're okay."

"The kids?" he gasped.

"The what?"

The driver of the car—a man about Dad's age, with his own crying kid in the backseat—lowered his window. He couldn't get out of the car. The door was stuck. "I didn't see them." He shook his head, face super pale. "They're so little. I didn't see them until they were right in front of the car. They ran right in front of me! If this kid hadn't pushed them out of the way . . ."

The mom rushed forward, pushing me aside as she kneeled next to Sam. "My babies!" she sobbed. "You saved them!"

I rocked back on my heels, but grabbed Sam's unhurt hand. He squeezed it, hard, and another moan fell out of him. My knees hurt again, the inside of my kneecaps twisting like worms. I squeezed back. "You're okay," I said. "It's all right." I used to be a lot better at lying. My voice shook and I ordered my eyes not to cry, but they didn't listen. I was so scared, like the accident still was happening.

Even as the ambulance came and the workers loaded Sam onto one of those stretchers, I held onto his hand.

Even as Mom, eyes fierce, ran toward me, Sam's mom right beside her, I held on. Mom wasn't wearing any shoes, I noticed in a daze. She only had on socks. "I heard the sirens, and I just knew I had to run," Mom said.

I only let go when one of the EMTs gently folded my fingers back from his hand.

Chapter Two

Mom wouldn't let me go in the ambulance with Sam, even though I swore I'd stay out of the way. She also wouldn't let me go to the hospital or even call him that night. I logged onto Roblox and waited all night to see him log on, too, but he never did. April came over and we just sort of sat side by side in my bedroom, not talking, until Mrs. Chester called and April had to go home. I wondered if Sam had to spend the night in the hospital.

The next morning, I was up before my baby sister, who screeches from her crib every morning just as the sun comes up. I sat in the hall outside her bedroom, waiting for our family's rooster to wake up Mom. But Dad was the one who stumbled down the hall when Molly started bellowing. "Lucy," he said mid-yawn. His face was scruffy and his breath sour. "What are you doing awake?"

I jumped to my feet. "Did you hear from Sam's family? Is he okay?"

Dad put his hand on my shoulder, pushing me back a little so he could open my sister's door. "I'm not sure we're going to hear anything today, Luce. The doctors and Sam's parents are pretty preoccupied right now." He went to Molly and lifted her from the crib.

My little sister was eight months old, and much less of a lump than she used to be. She pumped her fists in the air and kept on yelling, not even softening a bit once Dad held her and then laid her down on the changing table. Molly's little eyes were squished shut from how wide she stretched her mouth to scream. She wasn't what you would call a morning person.

Dad stretched out her legs in one hand, held her arms in the other, and blew raspberries all over Molly's round belly. And as quick as that, she was giggling. Molly never stayed mad long. Usually, her laugh is more contagious than lice, but today my face felt cemented into a frown.

"Morning," Mom said as she came into the room. Even though Molly was still on the changing table, fresh diaper only half on, she turned toward Mom, stretching her arms out like she was a flower and Mom was the sun. Dad quickly finished with the diaper and Mom pulled Molly onto her hip.

"Well?" I was seriously losing patience with these guys. "Have *you* heard from Sam's parents?"

"Not since late last night," Mom said sleepily. She kissed the top of my head, then nibbled on Molly's neck to make her giggle again. Mom cradled the back of Molly's head in her palm before it could flop backward. Molly was born with Down syndrome, which meant some parts of her work differently than with most people, including her neck muscles, which weren't all that strong yet. Too much giggling and twisting first thing in the morning could wear her out a little.

"And?" I yelled. Molly's face twisted into a squashed tomato. For someone so noisy, she sure was sensitive to other people's loud emotions.

Mom, Dad, and I winced as Molly sucked in all the air in the room. Her mouth opened in a silent scream that was three, two, one second away from blasting my eardrums. Dad to the rescue! He popped a pacifier into Molly's open mouth a moment before eruption.

"Phew," he said. "Should I round up another one for you, Lucy?"

"Mom!" I stomped my foot. "What did you hear?"

Mom patted my cheek. "Sam is going to be fine. He had surgery last night to set the broken bones in his arm. He'll come home from the hospital this afternoon."

"Surgery?" I whispered.

Mom handed Molly to Dad and wrapped her arms around me. "It was a bad break, honey. Sam did an incredibly courageous thing, but it's going to be a long recovery."

"But he's going to be fine, right?"

Mom nodded. I heard Dad click on the television in the living room. "Hey! Sam's on the news!"

I ran to the television. A newscaster was saying, "Ten-year-old Sam Righter is recovering at Autumn Grove Hospital from injuries sustained while saving twin toddlers from being hit by a car at a local playground." A picture of Sam appeared in the upper right side of the screen. Too bad it was the school picture from last year— Sam was looking down, his floppy curls covering most of his face, not even smiling.

"What a hero!" the newscaster said.

❖ ❖ ❖

Sam's arm was seriously screwed up. Even though the accident had been three days earlier, he still hurt a lot. I could tell right away when Mom finally took me to his house, just from seeing his face. Usually when Sam saw me, his chocolate-brown eyes sort of crinkled at the corners, and his mouth stretched in a super slow smile. But when Mom and I walked in, only the corner of Sam's mouth twitched.

His shoulder had popped out of place in the accident—that was why his arm looked so strange at the playground. Plus the bones above and at his elbow fractured. He had a huge red cast from his shoulder down to his knuckles. "It's a comminuted fracture," he said as I signed his cast. I made my name extra large since I figured only April, Amanda, Sheldon, and I would fill up the enormo space. I added a little drawing of a wolf, too. Probably should've practiced a sketch first, though, since it ended up looking like a spiky-legged llama. *Not a llama*, I wrote beside the wolf.

"What does comminuted mean?" I asked.

Sam shrugged.

"It means it's broken in several places," Mrs. Righter said as she put a tray of cookies and juice boxes on the ottoman next to the couch. She ruffled Sam's hair. "Need any painkillers?"

Sam shrugged again, and Mrs. Righter shook out a pill from a bottle in her pocket. She grabbed a juice box and started to pop in the straw. "Mom," Sam whined. "I can open a juice box."

"I know," she said, doing it anyway. She handed the juice box to Sam and tried to run her fingers through his hair, which looked, honestly, like he hadn't taken a shower in a few days. Not that I haven't been known to dodge a shower here or there, but Sam usually had gymnastics practice—and a shower—before school, so I was used to seeing his hair all floppy and clean, not dingy and sort of crusty looking. Sam twisted his head away from his mom's hand and took the pain pill and the juice. Mrs. Righter sighed and turned to Mom. "Do you want to grab a cup of coffee in the kitchen?"

"That would be lovely." But Mom couldn't seem to tear her eyes from Sam's cast. I saw her chin wobble. For the past two nights, I had heard Mom and Dad whispering after I went to bed about lots of "could've" and "what if" scenes where I was the one who had been hit by the car.

And, okay fine. After I found out that Sam was going to be all right, *I* spent time wondering what would've happened if I had been the one hit, too. I knew just how it would've gone down, too. I would've done this whirling dive thing where I pushed the twins out of the way—they'd fly through the air sort of slow motion like and land in the sandpit. The car would hit me—also in slow motion—and I'd crumple onto the hood. My pack would gather around me. "No!" Sam would scream. "Why couldn't it have been me? Why couldn't it have been me?"

Amanda would've held poor sobbing Sheldon close, shielding his eyes from the destruction, and April would swear that she would come back to Autumn Grove Intermediate immediately if I would just open my eyes.

And then, of course, I would. But not until the television crews and newspaper reporters arrived on the scene.

"Why are you smiling and waving? And your eyes are closed. It looks creepy." We'd only been at Sam's house for about ten minutes and already it was pretty obvious: broken bones made Sam cranky.

I shrugged and snagged a cookie from the tray since Sam's politeness also seemed to be fractured and he hadn't offered me one yet. "Just imagining what it must be like to be in newspapers and on the TV." I nudged his good shoulder. "I bet they make a movie about you!"

Sam half laughed. "I hope they get someone famous to play me."

"No way, dude!" I said, chomping on the cookie. Something sharp, like a sideways potato chip, shifted in my throat when Sam smiled. "We're going to play ourselves! Can you imagine, the pack in Hollywood?" I practiced some poses. "You should work on your auto-graph." I handed him the marker I had just used to sign his cast.

"I'm not signing my own cast. That's pretty pathetic, even for us." Sam doodled on it, though, drawing a pretty awesome wolf next to my not-so-awesome wolf.

"Good thing you broke your left arm," I pointed out. "So how long until it's healed?"

Sam dropped the marker and let his head fall back on the couch, staring up at the ceiling. He shifted a little. That sharp feeling pricked at my throat again. "At least three months. And then I might need to have another surgery."

I glanced around the room, filled with balloons and flowers and cards.

"Another surgery?" Geez. Some guys have all the luck. "So have you heard from the twins? Are you, like, their hero now?"

Sam shrugged. Seeing how that little movement made him wince did that funky thing to my knees again—making them feel all liquidy. Okay, so maybe there were some downsides to having a broken arm. Sam grumbled, "I heard they had a few stitches. One of them might have a concussion." I glanced at Sam's forehead. The curls mostly hid the butterfly bandage over the gash.

"Oh," I said. "I'm sure it's not as bad as a grapefruit concussion, eh?" I thought that would at least get a laugh again, but Sam just twisted his lips together. "Oh, come on, Sam! Soon you'll be back to normal."

For a long time, Sam didn't say anything. When he finally did speak, it was super quiet, the way he spoke before we were a pack. I leaned in to hear him. "I don't think so."

"Of course you will be. You'll be flipping around on the rings and that horse thing in no time! I can see it now. The final scene of your movie: You win Olympic gold!"

I guess the painkillers still weren't working because Sam's chocolate-brown eyes watered.

Mrs. Righter and Mom came back in the room. "We should get going, Lucy," Mom said. "I'm sure Sam wants to rest." Sam barely said bye as I left, just sort of waved with his good hand and stared toward the television.

As we were leaving, Mom picked up the newspaper on the Righters' front stoop. "Hey, look!" she said to Mrs. Righter, who had walked us to the door. "Sam's in the paper!"

"Oh!" Mrs. Righter's face brightened. "I was wondering if they'd run something today. A reporter came by yesterday to interview Sam. Let's show him! Might cheer him up a bit."

We followed her back into the house. I sat back down next to Sam on the couch as Mrs. Righter shook out the paper. "Check it out, Sam!" I said. "You're famous!"

The whole top of the newspaper—aside from a little column on the right about another bicycle theft—was a huge picture of Sam on the couch, the fireplace mantle lined with trophies just behind him, his broken arm stretched out in front of him. (If only I had signed the cast earlier!) A small picture to the side of the article was from his last gymnastics meet, on the pommel horse. The big headline over the top of the story read: LOCAL BOY SAVES TWINS AT PARK . In smaller print under that, a second headline read: ENDS GYMNASTICS CAREER.

"W-what?" I stammered.

"Oh, Sam." Mrs. Righter sucked in her breath.

"Seems odd to pin a career on a ten-year-old," Mom murmured.

Sam dropped the paper. I snagged it from his lap, smoothing it across my legs.

Sam Righter, 10, of Autumn Grove saved twin toddlers at a local playground Tuesday. He pushed them away as a car approached, taking the hit himself instead. In the process, the fifth-grade gymnast effectively ended his competitive future.

"But you're only going to be in a cast for a couple months. Then you'll go right back to racking up trophies."

Mrs. Righter's eyes darted to Sam, who stared at the juice box in his hand. "I'm afraid it's not that simple." She chewed her lip.

"But—but . . ." I didn't know a lot about gymnastics, but I knew Sam was a pretty big deal at his gym. He went to this gymnastics camp in Stanford over the summer. By the end of it, he said he was on the brink of going from a level seven to eight. I wasn't exactly sure what that meant, aside from him spending a lot more time at practice and going to more meets. More trophies for the already-crowded mantle, too. But I knew he was pretty proud of it.

Quietly, Mrs. Righter said, "Sam's going to miss the entire competitive season. The team is sponsoring a different gymnast now."

I felt my eyebrows cinch together in the middle—the way they always do when I'm trying to make sense out of things that don't make sense. "But once he's better, he'll be back on the team, right?" We were talking about Sam like he wasn't in the same room, unbroken arm practically pressed against mine. But he was so quiet that it almost felt like he wasn't there.

I even jumped a little when he spoke, his voice cold. "I'm going to have to start over. Work back up to level eight from scratch."

Mrs. Righter sighed. "Sam . . ."

My friend twisted his head away.

"We should get going," Mom murmured.

"But you'll get there!" I touched Sam's fingers. "You love gymnastics."

"Lucy—" Mom gave me the one-eyebrow-raised you-need-to-be-quiet look.

"The thing is," Mrs. Righter said softly, "the doctors don't think Sam's arm will ever be as strong as it was. The strain from gymnastics—even at a lower level—could cause permanent damage, even after the cast is off. We can't risk that. So . . ."

"So no more gymnastics," I finished for her. I sat back against the couch, feeling Sam slump slightly away from me. Mom held out her hand for me, but I ignored it for a moment. I thought about all that Sam had gone through for this sport that he loved—and not just the before- and after-school practices, missing summer camp together, and the physical working-until-you're-a-sweaty-mess stuff. I knew he iced his knees almost every day. I thought about the uglier things, too. Like being picked on by the kids at school who thought it was a "girly" sport, who asked him about his leotards and things like that. Like what Henry and Tom did to him last year, hanging him by his underpants in the locker room, just because they were jealous when he showed off a little on the monkey bars.

The newspaper slid off our laps onto the floor as I stood. At the bottom of Sam's story, there was a picture of the twins on their mom's lap. Underneath it was a quote from the mom: "Sam Righter is a hero!"

Mom and I didn't say anything as Mrs. Righter led us to the front door. "He'll be all right," Mom promised Mrs. Righter, who didn't look so sure.

As the screen door closed behind us, a huge van with satellite dishes and the name of the local news station pulled up in front of Sam's house.

Mom wouldn't listen to me when I said we should stay for Sam's interview. I could've held his hand while they asked him questions. Sam hates answering questions.

(When we gave our speech on wolves last year, I did most of the talking because whenever Ms. Drake talked to him directly he got sweaty and pale and held his stomach.) Maybe I could've even given a first-person account of the accident! She dragged me to the car.

I just hoped Sam wasn't so bummed about gymnastics to not appreciate all the news reports. I mean, this was Sam. Sam! Whatever he did instead of gymnastics would be equally awesome.

Man, what I wouldn't give to be a hero!

Chapter Three

Becky, my used-to-be best friend, turned arch nemesis, turned someone-I-sort-of-say-hi-to-once-in-a-while-but-mostly-avoid, stood at the bus line on the first day of school. More specifically, at *Sam's* bus line. "What are you doing here?" I asked. "Shouldn't you be in class?"

Becky fluffed her red curls. "Shouldn't *you* be?" Her lips, weighed down with about an inch of ChapStick, smacked together when she spoke.

"I'm waiting for Sam." I crossed my arms. "I'm going to carry his bags since his arm is so messed up."

"Go back to your locker, Lucy. I was here first."

"What? You're not even friends with Sam."

"Of course I'm friends with Sam." Becky rolled her

eyes like I was the stupidest person alive. My foot really wanted to kick her in the shin, so I stomped it instead.

"You and jerkface Tom and egg-breath Henry made his life miserable last year! You're *not* his friend. *I'm* his friend."

The bus pulled up and groaned to a stop in front of us. Becky elbowed me in the ribs and stepped on my foot. "Back off, Lucy!"

"You back off," I snapped, pushing her out of my way.

"Sam! Sam!" Becky called, bouncing up on her shoes and waving her arms like maybe he also broke his eyeballs or something.

Sam was the last one off the bus; three other people squeezed by where Becky and I stood, side by side with elbows out—and maybe poking into a rib or two. Sam paused at the top of the bus steps, holding out his giant red cast across his body. His eyes widened as I leaped forward and held out my hand. "Give me your bag, Sam!"

"Why?" He didn't move.

"No!" Becky yelped. And can you believe it? She pulled my hair! Seriously, grabbed my ponytail and yanked it backward so hard it actually moved me back a few inches! "Give *me* your bag, Sam!"

Click, click, click. I knew those footsteps. Those belonged to Ms. Drake, my fourth-grade teacher, making a speedy line toward me and Becky.

"*I'm* helping Sam," I snapped. "Go away, Becky."

"No, *I'm* helping Sam!" She still had my hair in her fist. I don't know how it happened, but somehow my foot got what it wanted and *bam*, it smacked against Becky's shin.

"Lucy!" Sam shouted at the same time I was again pulled from behind! Not by my hair this time, but by my shoulder.

"Lucy Beaner, did I just see you kick another student?" Ms. Drake's angry eyes nailed me in place.

I bit my lip, thinking fast. "I tripped."

Ms. Drake's nostrils flared and her eyes narrowed. "Is that so, Becky?" she asked but kept her eyes locked on mine.

"Yes," I quickly answered for Becky. "I tripped after she *accidentally* pulled my hair. Right, Becky?"

Becky huffed. "I'm just helping my friend with his bag since his arm is broken."

Ms. Drake turned to Sam. "Mr. Righter, are you capable of handling your own bag, considering it's the first day of school and said bag is likely empty of everything except a folder and some pencils?" A crowd of people had formed around us. They laughed at Ms. Drake's words.

"Yes, Ms. Drake," Sam mumbled. His face flamed. Sam hated being laughed at. He hated having people look at him. Sam spent most of fourth grade trying to be practically invisible. "I didn't ask them to—"

"Get to class, all of you!" Ms. Drake clapped her angry hands.

"See you later, Sam!" Becky twirled away and practically skipped toward the school doors.

My friend finally trudged down the stairs, his shoulder knocking me as he passed. "Thanks a lot, Lucy."

I threw my hands up and let them slam down on my sides. I couldn't believe this! Sam was blaming me for Becky picking a fight? I glared at his back as he disappeared into the swarm of students. A lot of them slapped him on the back. A few even called out, "Hey, Sam!" like he wasn't in a pack of dorks with me. Not that Sam appreciated any of the attention. Even with his back turned, I could tell his face was burning red because of how the back of his neck was splotchy. He hunched over and kept his head down.

I shook my head. "I can't believe him. Such lack of gratitude."

Ms. Drake cleared her throat.

"Oh!" I yelped. "We're going to be late to class!"

"Yes, you are." She crossed her arms.

"We better hurry!"

"Yes, you'd better." Over the summer, Ms. Drake went from being a fourth-grade teacher to the principal. I guess that was why she could loiter around in the bus line at the beginning of school. I guess that was also why she upped her game in the intimidating stares. Last year, she sometimes looked like a turtle, staring us all down with her neck stretched out. This year, she looked more like a dragon. Her lips were pressed so hard together they were white. Maybe that was because if she opened them, fire would come out and no one wanted a fire drill on the first day of school.

"Why are you staring at me, Lucy, instead of getting to class?" she asked with her teeth tightly clenched.

"Going! Going!" I turned and rushed toward the doors before Ms. Drake could dragon-breathe me.

"Wrong way, Ms. Beaner!" Ms. Drake called out before the door shut behind me.

I opened the door and peeked out at her. She jabbed her finger in the opposite direction of where I was headed. "But all the fifth-grade classrooms are to the right," I said. Silly, Ms. Drake. Did she forget I wasn't in her class anymore?

Ms. Drake shook her head again. "*Most* of the fifth-grade classrooms are to the right. You have Miss Parker for homeroom. Her class abuts the library."

"It does what to the library?"

"Abuts." Ms. Drake sighed. "It means adjacent."

"Oh," I said, holding open the door with just my foot. It felt safest this way, keeping Ms. Drake visible through just the crack. "I'd stick with adjacent, if I were you."

❖ ❖ ❖

The library spanned most of the hall, and the farther I walked down it, the quieter it got. It felt like someone dropped a thick quilt over this part of the school, muffling all of the chaos and chatter that had flooded my ears when I first stepped inside the school. Maybe part of that was because I was really late at this point and most kids already were sitting at their desks on the whole opposite side of the school. All I heard was the squelch of my new sneakers against the plasticky floor.

Even stranger, when I finally reached our classroom (all the way at the end of the hall by the emergency exit), my new teacher wasn't even there. I scooted through the door. The only seat left was smack dab in the middle, right in front of Miss Parker's empty one. I glanced around at all the strangers around me. (They weren't really strangers—Autumn Grove is a pretty small town and hardly anyone new ever moves here. But none of these guys were in my pack so they felt like strangers.)

"Hey, Lucy," Lily, the girl next to me, said. At least, I think that was what she said. She sneezed when she said my name and it came out sounding like Lisa. But, as I said, everyone knows everyone in Autumn Grove so I knew it was just the sneeze talking. Thankfully she didn't spray, if you know what I mean.

"Hey," I said. Lily was sort of friends with everyone. "Have you met Miss Parker yet?"

"Yeah, I saw her in the office last week when Mom dropped off my inhaler at the nurse. She's really young and pretty."

And lazy, apparently. I knew we were in fifth grade now and more mature, but still, I was pretty disappointed by the boring blank walls. Last year, Ms. Drake had colorful wallpaper on the boards around the room and curtains hanging from the windows. This room was stark and bare. It looked like Miss Parker hadn't gotten around to doing anything more than stapling posters at the top of the boards. They were still rolled up. The blinds were pulled to the ceiling. The whole room was white and boring. And where was the teacher?

"Should we, I don't know, call the office?" Lily wondered aloud.

"Seriously? This is awesome. No teacher, no problems," said an all-too-familiar voice.

I whipped around in my seat, hoping my ears had mistaken me. Nope. There in the back corner was none other than King Jerkface of the Kingdom Jerkface, Tom Lemmings. He smirked at me. I narrowed my eyes, trying to beam through to him all the inappropriate and mean names that popped in my mind the moment I saw his chicken-skin face and stupid red ears. My foot badly wanted to do some more kicking. *No*, I told myself. *We won't submit to violence twice in one morning. We're better than that.* But still, if anyone needed a kick in the shin, it was Tom Lemmings.

A buzzing sound diverted our glare-off. A walkie-talkie rattled on the middle of Miss Parker's otherwise empty desk. "Pschaw-pschaw! Agent Parker, do you read?" a gravelly voice called out on the other end.

Suddenly there was a banging, like something

slamming against the lockers in the hall. Lily gasped and covered her mouth. I jumped to my feet, ready for . . . I didn't know what. But I was ready!

Then, from the hall, I heard, "Agent Coulson, mission complete. Over and out."

"No way!" Tom huffed.

In walked, I guessed, Miss Parker. She stepped in the doorway, shoving a walkie-talkie in her pocket. Lily had been right: Miss Parker was young. In fact, she could've been babysitter age. Her hair was orangey red and hung flat down her back. Thick bangs went in a straight slash across her forehead. She wore makeup. A lot of makeup. But not in the cakey way a lot of Grandma's friends wear makeup. Miss Parker's brown eyes were surrounded by thick black eyeliner that stretched out from the corner of her eyes. Her eyebrows were just as dark as her black eyelashes despite her regular hair being orange. She wore a polka-dotted buttoned shirt and narrow black skirt with super high heels. And here's the oddest part: a cape. Like a shiny, red, button-under-the-neck cape.

"What—" Lily started.

"Oh!" Miss Parker smiled. Her lips were bright red with lipstick. "Never mind this, okay?" She unsnapped the cape and whipped open a desk drawer to shove the cape inside. "Sorry I was late, students."

Her eyes snagged on the walkie-talkie. "Did I—" She glanced toward us. Miss Parker swept up the walkie-talkie, twisting a knob on top to make sure it was turned off. "Please disregard anything you heard from this device. I'm sure it was picking up neighborhood chatter. Certainly nothing with which you need to be concerned."

I glanced around again. Everyone stared, open-mouthed, at this teacher who looked *nothing* like a teacher. Except, unlike me, they were all sitting in their seats. Quickly I slid into mine.

"So." Miss Parker folded her hands in front of her. "Let's get to know each other, shall we?" She nodded as if we had agreed, and then moved around the room, pulling down the rolled-up posters. The first was a giant cityscape at night, stretching across a whole wall. "I love cities," she said as she stapled the poster in place. "Living in them, visiting them, protecting them, helping them."

"Protecting?" Lily whispered.

A small white cord snaked out from the corner of the poster. Miss Parker wedged it into a light socket and flipped a little switch. Suddenly the poster lit up!

It must've had hundreds of little lights embedded in it. Everyone gasped like they'd never seen a Christmas tree. The next poster was covered in huge speech bubbles like you'd see in a comic book. Inside the bubbles were phrases, including *My favorite place is . . . My bravest moment was . . . I'm best known for . . .* and *My hero emblem looks like . . .* As she stapled it in place, Miss Parker said, "Every week, we'll highlight another student's superlatives, or extra special aspects, here."

The next poster was exactly the same except all the blanks were filled in with information from Miss Parker. Her favorite place was *Gotham City*. Her bravest moment was *teaching fifth grade*. Her hero emblem was a diamond with a giant *P* in the middle, painted in red and gold. The strangest was what she's best known for—next to that she wrote *LARPing*. What the heck was LARPing? Were we going to have go LARPing? I didn't know what it was but it sure sounded like farting and burping at the same time to me. Regardless of what LARPing was, I was pretty sure my parents wouldn't be okay with it.

"You might already have guessed this last bit." Miss Parker laughed.

Tom laughed, too, only not in his usual snorty laughing-at-not-with way. "Cool," he said.

Wait. What? Tom knew something I didn't? This was unacceptable.

"Who else is a fan of LARPing?"

Of course, jerkface Tom's hand shot in the air. Mine did, too. I swear I didn't have full limb control today. First, my foot kicking Becky. Now my hand shooting in the air. At any moment, my elbows might break out in the cha-cha.

"Wonderful," Miss Parker grinned. I swear, the light through the windows glinted across her perfect white teeth. "What do you LARP as, Lucy?"

How did she already know my name?

"Oh, you know. I just LARP. All the time, I'm LARPing," I said. Grandma has this saying: Fake it till you make it or break it. I was full-on going to fake LARP. My stomach rumbled a little as if to say it was in, too.

"Really?" Miss Parker's eyebrow popped up. "As what?"

As what? "Um, you know. As much as I can."

Miss Parker's face tilted. Tom laughed.

His hand shot up. "Yes, Tom," Miss Parker said.

"Lucy's right. She's awesome at LARPing."

Wait. What? King Jerkface was standing up for me? What was happening? The world had ceased to make sense.

"Yeah, I mean, look at her! She's LARPing right now as a"—snort, snort, snort—"Super Dork." Other people joined in, snickering around the classroom.

I jumped to my feet again.

"Watch out!" Tom said. "She's going to split her skirt again!"

"Stop it!" I yelled. Or I would've yelled it, but someone beat me to it. Miss Parker wasn't yelling exactly, but it was like her sweet voice turned sharp enough to cut right through Tom's snorts. His face paled even as I felt mine burn. "Tom is demonstrating unacceptable behavior. Never in this classroom will we ridicule or demean another person. *Never*. Fix it, Tom."

"Fix it?" he and I repeated together.

"Yes." Miss Parker stared at Tom.

He swallowed and shifted in his seat. "Sorry," he said.

"Not forgiven," I replied, lowering into my seat.

"You're not done yet. Fix it," Miss Parker repeated.

Staring at his shoes, Tom muttered, "I shouldn't have said that, Lucy. I'm sorry. You're not a Super Dork."

"That was better," said Miss Parker before I could once again tell Tom he was not forgiven. "Throughout the year, we'll work on proper apologies, including looking someone in the eye. We'll also discuss graceful acceptance of apologies." Her eyes slid to me, burning a hole in the top of my head. I wouldn't look up. No way. And no way was Tom forgiven.

"Do you hear me, Lucy?"

I grunted.

"For now, let's move on." Miss Parker addressed the whole class. "LARPing, of course, stands for Live Action Role Playing, where we can take on the persona of a superhero or villain. I think my favorite part about being a superhero is the way they just take charge. When they see someone needs help, they charge ahead, just the way any of us would for one of our friends."

I squirmed in my seat, thinking of the moment I saw Sam folded up on the pavement, and how the rest of the pack rushed forward while my knees went hollow and wouldn't move.

Miss Parker continued, "I suppose that's why I love to LARP! I even go to conventions and meetings. Some people are even convinced I'm a *real* superhero. Isn't that fun?" I peeked up, just in time to see her wink. She *winked*.

Did she really think we'd fall for this? An extra walkie-talkie that just happens to be turned on. A cape accidentally left around her shoulders. Knowing all of our names. Did she think that's all it would take to convince us all she was a superhero?

Miss Parker moved throughout the room, lowering blinds to reveal pictures of all of the Avengers all across them and stapling Wonder Woman in place along the back wall until all surfaces in the classroom sparkled and everyone in the class was cheering. Everyone except me and Tom, that is.

"This year, we're going to focus a lot on the superpowers we all have—powers like truth, honesty, and bravery. We're going to dig deep and be brave. We're going to fight for justice!" She shook a fist in the air, revealing a thick gold-band bracelet. *Dig deep and be brave?* Can't we just be regular fifth graders? I closed my eyes, but my brain again replayed that moment the rest of my pack sprang into action for Sam while I turned to liquid.

"That was *awesome*," Lily whispered a minute later when Miss Parker told us to get packed up for math class. We switched classrooms for math and science, but would begin each day with Miss Parker for homeroom and then end it with her after lunch, when she would teach writing and reading. In between, we'd have specials. The other classroom was on the whole other side of the building, in the regular fifth-grade wing. Maybe Miss Parker could work on giving us all super speed.

"What was awesome?" I whispered back.

"The way she handled you and Tom. She might actually be a superhero!"

I rolled my eyes. Miss Parker might've nailed Tom for being rude for once but she was no way a genuine superhero. Superheroes wouldn't be hard on the victim—me!—the way she had been. And that superlative chart? Only someone so actressy would create that. *The bravest thing I've done is . . .*

Um . . . once I took a shower knowing there was a spider in the stall, and neither of us died. (Actually, the spider fell down the drain, so it probably died. But I didn't have proof.)

Again, my mind fluttered to that moment when Sam was crumpled and I couldn't move. I guessed Sam wouldn't have to think too hard about when he had been brave. But me? I wasn't brave enough to be a hero. I wasn't even brave enough to be a Super Dork. Hopefully Miss Parker wouldn't fill out the chart in alphabetical order, so I'd time to actually do something before it was my turn.

Chapter Four

I was late to lunch since I had to run all the way past the cafeteria and then past the library to the lockers outside Miss Parker's classroom for my lunch bag.

Sheldon and Amanda already had been at our table, divvying up their lunches. Sheldon was reenacting the comet strike that demolished the dinosaurs, using Amanda's apple as the comet and his animal crackers as the dinosaurs. "Boom!" Amanda said as Sheldon smooshed the crackers. They high-fived and stared a smidgen too long at each other.

"Hey, Shemanda." I sighed as I pulled out a chair.

"Hey," they said together.

"Where's Sam?" I looked at the lunch line. If he was buying, he'd need help carrying his lunch tray. But there was Becky twirling her hair and standing right beside Sam. My Sam! *She* carried his tray, even though Sam said a few times that he could do it himself just fine.

"Oh, no!" Becky said as she approached our table. "It looks like there's only one seat left. Sam and I will sit somewhere else."

"No!" I jumped to my feet. "Sit here, Sam."

"No, Sam," Becky said, her eyes on me, though. "Over there!"

Sam took a deep breath and sat down. "I'll see you later, Becky."

She huffed but finally walked off. I wiggled my fingers good-bye when I thought Sam wasn't looking and she stuck her tongue out at me. "Knock it off," Sam muttered.

"She started it."

"I hate this," Sam said, resting his cast across his lap. "Everyone's looking at me."

"Do you want some help?" I asked. "I could cut up the noodles."

"No!" Sam pushed aside my hand when I reached for his tray. His tone softened a little. "I've got to figure out how to do this stuff on my own."

Sheldon leaned over and fake punched Sam in his good shoulder. "Enjoy, bud. You're massively popular right now."

I glanced around. Sure enough, people from other tables were looking our way, whispering and pointing. This, frankly, wasn't a new experience for me. Or Sam. Or Shemanda. But this was different. I couldn't quite put my finger on how their expressions were different. Oh, that's right. They weren't mocking us.

"Wow," I said and turned back to my peanut butter and jelly.

"Yeah, Sam," Amanda said, "you could even run for class president. I know you'd win."

Before we left her room that morning, Miss Parker reminded us about the upcoming elections and pointed to the stack of applications on her desk. I laughed a little to myself, thinking about Sam as class president. He'd be awesome at it, no doubt, but he'd hate every single second—campaigning, talking to people, making speeches. He'd probably rather break off his arm entirely.

"Um, excuse me." Lily stood just behind us.

"Oh, hey," I said. "What's up?"

Lily's eyebrow arched. "I didn't see you there, Lisa," she said.

"Lucy," I corrected. "I'm Lucy. I sit directly behind you in homeroom."

"Right," Lily said and turned so her back was to me. "Sam, I was wondering. Could I sign your cast?"

"Oh. Um, sure." Sam's face was as bright red as his cast. "I don't have a pen or—"

But Lily popped the cap off a Sharpie with her teeth and grabbed Sam's arm. She scrawled, *To a real hero, Lily*. Puke alert: the *i* was topped with a heart. "Is it true that you held those twins above your head as the truck crashed into you?"

"No," Sam said.

"But you threw them in front of you, right?"

"Yeah, I guess so," he muttered. "It happened really fast, I don't remember."

Amanda snorted. "Being knocked unconscious will do that to you."

"You were there?" asked Lily, looking up at Shemanda.

"Of course we were," I butt in. "We're a pack." Sheldon growled and Amanda sort of yipped but Sam didn't say anything.

Lily put the cap back on the pen. "But you three didn't do anything?"

"Four," Amanda said. "April was there, too."

"They did stuff," Sam said. His ears were red now, too. His face was so steaming that a splotch of spaghetti sauce near his cheek barely stood out. "Sheldon and Amanda called 9-1-1. April got ahold of my mom."

"What about you, Lisa?" Lily turned toward me.

"*Lucy*," Sam started, "Lucy, well, she . . ."

Sam shifted to face me, I guess hoping I'd pipe in with something great I had done. I saw instead how big and stupid my signature on his cast looked now that a dozen other names were written right over it. Again, I closed my eyes and saw Sam crumpled on his side. Saw everyone else rush toward him. Felt my knees go hollow and squiggly all at once.

"I didn't do anything."

❖ ❖ ❖

The pack had plans to meet at the park after school. Since I pass April's house, I stopped there so we could walk together. Though it had taken Mrs. Chester a few minutes to find April over the chaos of all the other kids running around their house, eventually April came prancing down the stairs. It always startled me lately to see April. Gone was the frizzy hair and sniffly nose. In the past six months, she had discovered three things that seemed to have changed her entirely: martial arts, hair conditioner, and a non-zombifying allergy medicine.

Her hair now fell in super soft, pretty waves down her back. The allergy medicine meant she could breathe with her mouth shut and helped her break her disgusto nose-picking habit (in fact, she even painted her nails pretty colors now). Learning martial arts had changed her, too. She just carried herself differently now. Not in a might-slap-your-face-off-at-any-moment way like Amanda. But in an I'm-perfectly-capable sort of way. April also looked way older in her school uniform—a black pleated skirt, white collared shirt, and my old penny loafers. (I was obsessed with them last year. But this year I needed a new look, so I passed them on to her when I heard Mrs. Chester say they'd have to wait until the second week of school, when Mr. Chester got paid, to get her new shoes. Money's kind of tight at her house, with all the kids. It's not like my parents have a lot, but Grandma had taken me back-to-school shopping and I had two new pairs of sneakers and knew I'd never wear the loafers again anyway.)

"Oh, hey, Lucy!" April said.

"Hey, April, ready to go to the park?" I asked.

Scrappy, April's four-year-old little brother, zoomed around the corner only to stand just beside me. He grinned, making it obvious he had been spying on us. "That's a great idea. Let's go to the park." He crossed his arms and nodded as if I had been talking to him instead of April. "Yeah, park sounds great."

"Scrappy! Lucy's here to see me! Not you!" April whipped around and yelled up the stairs, "*Mom! Scrappy's following me again!*"

I smiled. This, at least, was the same. Whenever April was around her family, she slipped back into her old April-ish way of speaking—all bursts, all the time. With three little brothers and an older sister, all of the Chester kids had to shout to be heard.

"Scrappy doesn't bother me," I said. The little kid was kind of cute, huge brown eyes and super excited about absolutely everything. Plus it was kind of nice to have someone who always wanted to do exactly what you wanted to do, who thought every idea you had was awesome. I guess I could see how it'd get annoying if it were constant, like it was for April, but just then Scrappy's face practically split in half with a tremendous grin just because I said he didn't bother me.

"Fine," April said and crossed her arms. "But leave us alone, Scrappy. I want to tell Lucy all about school and I don't want you bugging us." To me, she added, "I'll be right back. I just want to change out of my uniform."

"I go to school, too, now," Scrappy said as soon as April turned away.

"Preschool is not school!" April shouted back down the stairs at him.

"Is so!" He stuck his tongue out at April's back. "It was my first day, too. I have a backpack with a duck on it and my teacher has a fire truck that's the size of my hand. The fire truck fits in my backpack with the duck on it. It likes my backpack. So it's mine."

"Did you steal a fire truck on your first day of school?"

"Let's talk about something else!" Scrappy put his hand in mine. It was sticky and cold but kind of nice anyway. "Do you have lunch at school or do you have to go home? Guppies have to go home. I'm a guppy. Sometimes guppies can join the dragonflies and stay for lunch but Mama says since I'll go to half-day kindergarten, I don't need the same practice that dragonflies have to have and I can come home and eat peanut butter and jelly and remember to use a napkin in my own home."

"Did you remember to use a napkin today?" I asked, and squiggled my fingers around Scrappy's sticky hand.

"No, I used my hands instead but I licked it all clean like a cat. I love cats."

I slipped my hand out from under Scrappy's and wiped it on my pants leg as he kept chattering.

I tuned back in as he asked, "Well, did *you*?"

"I used a napkin," I said.

"No, did you eat at school with your friends?"

"Oh," I said. "Yeah, I sat with my friends."

I rubbed the heels of my hands into my eyes, trying to scrub away the image of Sam on his side, forget the whole stupid lunch conversation and remember where I was, waiting for April with her little brother.

"Want to know what I did?"

"Aside from stealing a fire truck?"

"Let's talk about something else," Scrappy said. "Like we could talk about my new bike! Want to see it?"

"Sure," I said and followed him out the back door to their yard.

Scrappy ran, his arms pumping, toward a shed in the Chesters' yard. Soon he came pedaling out on a yellow bicycle. I recognized the bike—it used to be April's. When it had been hers, the basket on front had been covered with bright purple and pink plastic flowers. Scrappy had replaced them with action figures.

His little feet barely reached the pedals and the training wheels were the only thing keeping him upright. "Do you see me, April's friend? Do you see me biking?"

"I see you." I sat down on the bottom step of the back porch and waited for April. I wondered if the rest of the pack even remembered our plan to meet at the park. Sam hadn't planned on going—he usually had gymnastics practice right after school. But maybe now that his arm was screwed up, he'd have more time to hang around with us.

"Look!" Scrappy said. "I'm biking! I'm a bicycler! I bike!"

"You're doing great," I said, but I really was looking at my hangnail. Did you ever have one that poked out a little bit? I knew if I pulled it out it'd sting pretty bad, but if I didn't, it'd keep getting snagged whenever I put my hand through my jacket sleeve. Even worse if Mom noticed it and came at me with the clippers. Chewing on it seemed to be my best bet. But just when I gnawed it down to a proper nub, I remembered that this was the hand that Scrappy had held with his licked-clean hand. Yuck!

"I go fastest on the sidewalk," he called out. "Look!" Scrappy pedaled through the Chesters' gate and onto the sidewalk just as April swung open the back door.

"Scrappy!" she yelled and leaped over me. Right over me! She landed on her feet and tore off toward her little brother. I jumped to my feet. There was a big kid—a teenager—standing in front of Scrappy's bike. He had his hands on the handlebars and was jerking it back and forth, trying to shake Scrappy right off it!

"No, it's mine! It's mine!" Scrappy hiccupped.

"Getoffit!" the kid yelled like it was all one word. He shook the bike so hard, Scrappy slipped off it right onto the sidewalk. The kid whipped around, tucking the bike under his arm and ready to run off with it.

But he wasn't counting on April, who slammed the kid across the chest with a ridge hand hit. Her arm was like a whip—*bam!*—whapping the kid with a thunk that made his arms fly out and drop the bike. Without pausing, April swept out a low hook kick under the teenager's knees and lunged forward with a palm strike in the center of his chest, sending him crashing to the sidewalk.

Scrappy straightened the bike as April pressed her foot down on his chest. "Don't even think of moving," she growled.

A soft whimper slipped out of the teenager's mouth.

"That's right!" Scrappy bellowed. He kicked the teenager in the side of the shin, eliciting another whimper.

"Knock it off, Scrappy," April snapped. "Go get Mom."

But I was already on it.

This time, I didn't flake out. I ran into the house screaming louder than Grandma that time a bat flew into her car. "Help! Help!" I screeched. "April caught the bike thief! April caught the bike thief!"

Chapter Five

"So then Mr. Chester held down the teenager until the police got there," I finished telling the pack what had happened at April's house the day before. We were at the park, together at last. When I had finally gotten there the night before, everyone had already left. At school earlier, both Sam and Sheldon had stayed in their classroom at lunch to eat with Mr. Grayson, who had "lunch bunch" clubs once a week. And Amanda had spent all of lunchtime telling me about her dad's new job, which actually sounded pretty awesome, though she was (surprise) angry about it. So this was the first time I could really tell anyone about the adventure at April's the night before.

"Is April okay?" Sam asked. "Why isn't she here?"

"It's Thursday! Karate night, remember?" I said.

Sheldon, Amanda, and I were sitting on the swings, rocking back and forth more than actually swinging. Sam was sitting on a picnic bench nearby. I wondered if it was weird for him to be back at the park, but he seemed pretty regular. Aside from his grouchiness. He made a jerky sort of nod. Maybe hearing about April's karate made him think about how he was supposed to be at gymnastics. Or maybe a gnat flew up his nose.

"And April's not just okay. She's amazing," I said. "I mean, you should've seen her just totally take on this kid. Bam, bam, bam! He was down. The police were interviewing her when I left. They said they think this kid is part of a bike ring. You know all the bikes that have been stolen? They think he either did it himself, or he'll lead them to the rest of the thieves."

"Whoa," Sheldon murmured. "April's, like, a hero."

Amanda shot up from the swing. "See you guys later. I'm going home to see if the police found my bike yet!" Sheldon, of course, leaped from his swing just behind Amanda and the two of them took off toward Amanda's house.

"So," Sam said as we walked back toward town a few minutes later. "April's a hero, too."

"Too?" I echoed.

His face flushed. "That came out weird."

I shrugged. "Nah, you're right. I bet she had report-ers at her house, too."

"It's strange," Sam said, "all this attention."

"It's like you're famous."

"I'm not used to people wanting to be around me."

"I want to be around you." And then, because the words fell like bricks, I quickly added, "And so does the rest of the pack."

"Yeah, I know," Sam said. "But it feels a little like . . . like I'm suddenly popular. It was actually kind of a relief to stay in Mr. Grayson's room at lunch. No one was star-ing at me or asking to sign my cast." His eyes slid toward me. "Sorry for not giving you the heads-up that Sheldon and I weren't going to be there."

I shrugged. I guess I had been annoyed that Sheldon had told Amanda about lunch bunch but Sam hadn't told me. But it's not like Sam is supposed to tell me things like that. It's not like we're a couple the way Shemanda is a couple. Still, it was nice for him to say he was sorry. The annoyed feeling floated away.

"I was popular once," I said. "It stunk."

"You didn't think so at the time," Sam pointed out. "You were bummed when you had to sit at the solo-eaters' table with me."

I tried to laugh, but it got stuck in my throat and came out like a cough. He was right. When I went from being popular to being a dork overnight in fourth grade, it was awful. I felt so alone, convinced everyone was watching me all the time, like everything everyone thought about me had nothing to with me—the *real* me—at all. I glanced at Sam. Maybe that's what it's like, too, when you go suddenly from being a dork to being popular.

We reached the split, where Sam had to keep going straight toward his house and I would turn right to reach mine. We both sort of stopped, not ready to head home.

Sam kicked a rock and shoved his good hand straight down into his pocket. He ducked his head and stared at the sidewalk. "I don't know how to not be a gymnast."

"Oh, it's easy!" I said. "I've been doing it for ten years."

"Har har," Sam fake-laughed.

I shoved my hands in my pockets, too, trying to figure out what to do or say. Truth was, I didn't know what it was like to have something I was really awesome at taken away. I wasn't really outstanding at anything, so I never had experienced no longer being great, either.

"You weren't always awesome at gymnastics," I pointed out. "I mean, when you started, you were just okay, right?"

"I guess," Sam said slowly.

"But you worked hard and became great. So just do that again but different!" I clapped my hands. It was so simple. "Be awesome at a new thing."

"What are you even talking about?"

"We're going to figure this out. We're going to find a new thing. We're going to be awesome again." Or, in my case, just awesome. No need for the again.

"Are you talking about yourself in the plural again?"

"No! Well, maybe. But I'm also talking about you. Both of us, we're going to find our awesome." And maybe in the process, I'd become a hero.

Sam bit his lip. Then he scratched the back of his head, ruffling the brown curls.

"What?" I groaned. "Just say it."

"It's just, when you get ideas, bad things happen."

"What ideas? What bad things?"

Sam's eyebrow popped up. Okay, so maybe he was thinking about my plot to become popular again last year in fourth grade. Or perhaps the matchmaking I undertook at summer camp. Neither worked out as planned—sure, last year Sam ended up hanging from his underpants in the locker room, I split my sausage skirt in a fit of rage, and Sheldon nearly went T-Rex on some jerkfaces—but here we were, a pack. And while, yes, at camp, there was a stray grapefruit-induced concussion, a surprisingly epic hot-chocolate/egg fire, and one camp counselor fired, a match still did flourish—even though camp ended months ago, Grandma and Mr. Bosserman were still "going steady," as Grandma put it. "It all worked out right at the end," I reminded Sam.

He shook his head with a half smile. "Okay, fine. We'll find our awesome." Sam started to cross the road. "But, maybe . . ."

"Maybe what?"

Sam stopped, still turned away from me. "I feel like maybe this isn't something we can figure out together. I feel like it's something I have to figure out alone."

"Don't be ridiculous."

"I'm not." Sam turned toward me but kept his head down. "I mean, we're still a pack, of course. I just, I have a lot of stuff to figure out. What I want to do . . ."

"We're not even eleven," I snapped. "I think you've got time—"

"You don't get it," Sam sighed. He stepped backward, away from me. Just as he did, a news van—the same one that had been parked in front of Sam's house a few days earlier—slowed in front of us. "Not again," Sam groaned and jumped backward. I sidestepped so I was in front of him.

But when the driver lowered the window, he didn't want to interview Sam. He wanted directions to April's house.

❖ ❖ ❖

Grandma's old station wagon was in our driveway when I got home.

A sign of how much things have changed since this summer: this was a surprise. Usually, Grandma popped in all the time. But lately, we only saw her a couple of times a week and never on the weekends, which she'd either spend with Mr. Bosserman down in Pennsylvania or showing him around New England here.

Wow, she stopped by just to hear about how fifth grade is going! If anyone could help me make sense of the weirdness of these first two days, from Sam's sudden popularity to April catching a thief to Miss Parker being a LARPer, it'd be Grandma. She probably already knew my awesome. She'd probably known it for years and had just been waiting for me to be ready to hear all about it. I rushed into the house.

"Grandma!" I shouted.

"Lucy!" she echoed back from the kitchen.

"Gabaga!" answered Molly.

Mr. Bosserman stood in front of me, holding Molly like she was a skunk-porcupine crossbreed. "She's brutzing!" he said in his gruff way. Molly's head lunged forward and she smooshed her face back and forth against Mr. Bosserman's flannel shirt, saturating it in Molly drool.

"That's not brutzing," said Grandma, who understood Mr. Bosserman's Pennsylvania Dutch. "She's just talking."

"Bubaguk," Molly said. She pulled back her face and blinked at Mr. Bosserman.

"Sounds like she's speaking Dutch," I said.

"Are you Dutch, girlie?" Mr. Bosserman's hands flexed a little around my baby sister as he shifted to hold her closer. He tilted his head so his chin rubbed against her fluffy brown hair. Molly crammed her hand into her mouth. "You're not gretzy. You're just hungry, onest."

Mom came up from the basement with a load of laundry. "Lucy! How was Day Two?"

"School started this week?" Grandma walked into the living room, testing a drop of Molly's pukey formula by dabbing the bottle on the inside of her wrist. Her heavy silver bracelets clinked as she rolled her wrist.

Mr. Bosserman held Molly out toward her, but Grandma just popped the bottle into Molly's little mouth and turned away. Mr. Bosserman sighed and sat down on the couch, stiffly holding Molly. Her mouth widened around the bottle. "Gabala!" she screeched. Mr. Bosserman stood up again, and she went back to drinking the bottle.

Grandma winked at me. I didn't wink back. She hadn't stopped by to see how school was going for me. She didn't even remember that fifth grade had started!

Why was she here, then? Grandma asked Mom to put down the laundry and have a seat. She pointed at me, then at the seat next to Mom.

"I've got some news," Grandma said.

Mr. Bosserman coughed.

"*We*'ve got some news," she amended. Grandma's arms were crossed tightly across her chest. "I was going to wait until Greg was here, too, but Harold gets indigestion if he eats after five o'clock and the early bird special at Eloise's Diner ends at four so we'll just have to say it now."

"Oh my god." Mom covered her mouth with her hands. "You have cancer. How bad is it? What kind? When—"

"Grandma has cancer!" I yelped.

"Gababa!" Molly chirped around her bottle.

"I don't have cancer!" Grandma snapped. She threw up her hands. "Isn't it possible I might have *good* news?"

And that's when I saw it. Grandma's diamond ring. It was just like the one that jerkface Tom Lemmings gave me last year just before he destroyed my life.

Chapter Six

"You're getting married?" I gasped and sat back down next to Mom. "But you're *old*."

Grandma's beetle eyes narrowed behind her smudged-up glasses. Her mouth twisted and I knew fiery words were about to rain down on me so I squished my eyes. But Mr. Bosserman (oh, lollipop farts! Would I have to call him Grandpa now?) was the one who spoke. "We're tired of this *sometimes here, sometimes there* life. We're getting married, onest."

"Congratulations," Mom squeaked, "um, Dad."

Mr. Bosserman's eyebrows shot up almost to his hairline, which is saying something. "You don't have to call me that. Maybe, um, just Harold?"

"All right, Harold," I said, "let's get to the important stuff. When's the wedding?"

Mom patted my knee. "Lucy, I don't think *you* should be calling Mr. Bosserman Harold."

"Well, what am I supposed to call him, then?"

We both looked at Harold. He cleared his throat and looked down at Molly, so we did, too. "Gaga," she said.

"Gaga!" I repeated. "Molly's first word!"

"Lucy," Mom laughed. "Molly's only eight months old. She's not saying anything."

"But she could've. You don't know that. She said Gaga. She wants Harold to be Gaga." I bounced on the chair. "You're Gaga now," I told Mr. Bosserman. Er, Harold. The man who's going to be married to my grandma. Gaga.

"I don't want to be Gaga," Gaga said.

"Too bad. It's decided, Gaga."

"Quit calling me that, onest."

Molly turned her face away from the bottle. "Gaga," she said and grinned.

Mr. Bosserman's breath sucked in like a balloon being blown up in reverse. "I think she *is* calling me Gaga." He looked up at Grandma and then at Mom with wide eyes. "Her first word is my name!"

Mom walked over to Grandma and gave her a hug. "Congratulations," she said. She smiled at Mr. Bosserman over Grandma's shoulder. "Welcome to the family."

"So, Gaga." I settled in next to him on the couch. "Are you shipping the whole caboose to Grandma's apartment or just packing up what's in it?" Mr. Bosserman lived like a caveman in an old caboose in the woods of Camp Paleo, where I had been forced to spend two weeks of my summer.

"The caboose is staying put," he said, and he kept his eyes on Molly. Mom and Grandma got strangely quiet and still.

For a moment, none of us spoke. Only the sound of Molly sucking on her bottle filled the room. "You're moving to the *caboose*? In the *woods*?" I gasped.

"Not exactly," Grandma said.

"We're going to see the country, don't you know?" When Mr. Bosserman said this, it came out like *doncha-now*.

Grandma cleared her throat. "When we told Alan about our plans to get hitched, he gave us an early present. An RV."

"A what?" I gasped.

"An RV. A motor home."

"That was . . . incredibly generous of Alan," Mom

said, and her voice was quiet, which usually meant her thoughts were loud.

"Oh, don't get your panties in a bunch," Grandma said, making Mom flinch. "We'd just be traveling for a year or so."

For a moment, I lost track of the whole ridiculousness of Grandma not living near me and got snagged a bit on a second thought. A huge thought. That *Alan* Grandma mentioned? That was Alan Bridgeway—tech genius, multimillionaire, and Mr. Bosserman's son. Alan Bridgeway was about to be my . . . Well, I wasn't really sure. What is the son of your step-grandfather? My uncle, maybe? Alan Bridgeway was going to be my uncle!

"Okay, so that was nice of Alan, but Grandma lives here. We need her here." I clapped my hands together now that this was decided. "But quick question: should I give my Christmas list to you or should I call Uncle Alan?" Everyone ignored me.

Grandma sat on the couch next to me. "It's just going to be for a year."

"No."

"Maybe this summer you, Molly, and your folks can fly out to wherever we'll be then and visit us." Her voice was gentle and not very Grandma-like.

"We'll be at the Grand Canyon in December," Mr. Bosserman said.

"He's got the whole trip mapped out already," Grandma said to Mom with a laugh. Mom just nodded without speaking.

"Alan outfitted that dang RV with GPS. Waste of money. Nothing beats a map. 'Specially when you've got a co-navigator." He winked at Grandma.

She laughed again. "Better stick with the GPS. I've never been anywhere but here and down to that camp of yours."

Mom took a deep breath through her nose. "Well, that's about to change, huh?" Now her voice was too bright. It was her I've-made-a-decision-to-be-happy voice.

I hated that voice.

I hated RVs and printed maps, and I hated rich maybe-uncles who gave thoughtful, generous gifts. I hated old farts who married grandmas and took them away even though they were just named Gaga by their grand-baby. I hated grandmas who showed up almost every day and then fell in love and got married anyway. I hated best friends who became heroes and friends who jumped into action and friends who got wrapped up in each other and everyone else who was leaving me behind. I hated everyone.

And I hated myself most of all for these ugly thoughts that grew and stretched and stood to shake themselves off inside of me until they were the only things I felt.

"When are you planning on going on this trip?" Mom asked in the same stupid too-high voice.

"Not until after we're hitched," Mr. Bosserman said.

"We were thinking of an autumn wedding." Grandma's heavy hand landed on my knee. She squeezed. "What do you think? Want to be the flower girl?"

"What do I think?" I echoed. And then the ugly monster took over my mouth. "What I think is: why wait? Get married today. Leave tomorrow. Leave before you ask me how school is. Spoiler alert: it's awful. Leave before Molly has a chance to remember who you are or the names she gave you. Leave." Somehow I was on my feet. "Why are you even asking what I think? You don't care! And I don't, either." And suddenly I was stomping down the hall. Even as I thundered away, I felt the ugly monster dissolve, turn into wispy shameful smoke.

But it left with a bang, the sound of my bedroom door slamming.

❖ ❖ ❖

Maybe it was an hour later. Maybe it was just a couple minutes.

A metallic clack knocked against my door and I knew Grandma was whapping one of her many rings against it and about to walk in. I rolled onto my side away from her. Grandma's sigh floated over me like a blanket. The bed groaned when she eased onto the mattress, and I dipped toward her, warm and soft, whether I wanted to do or not.

"You're wrong, kid," she whispered. The words fluffed wisps of my hair around my ear. "And I don't just mean about me not caring. You're wrong to think *you* don't care. That's why this upsets you so much. You think I'm choosing Harold over you."

"Well, you are, aren't you?" I rolled to face her.

"No." Grandma smiled up at the ceiling. "I'm choosing me. For the first time in a long time—maybe ever—I'm choosing me."

"What do you mean?"

"Harold makes me happy. I make him happy. We don't have a lot of years left, but we're going to spend them together, being happy. And if I thought for one second," Grandma held up her thick pointer finger as she said this, "that you needed me here more than you needed to see me take charge of my own life, then I'd stay."

I plopped back on my back, even though Grandma took up so much of the bed that a quarter of my body hung over the edge of the mattress. "But I *do* need you."

"And you'll have me," Grandma said. "I'll always be just a FaceTime away, and I can knock you upside that noggin of yours wherever I am." She kissed the top of my head, right above my ear.

"I'm glad you're happy," I said, a little louder.

Grandma took a deep breath, like my words were fresh air. "Don't wait until you're my age, toots, to go after what you want. It's scarier when you're set in your ways."

I wondered then how long Grandma had waited to fall in love. How long she had wanted something more than just knocking us all upside our noggins. "What if I don't know what I want?" But even as I asked, I realized I did know.

What is the bravest thing you've ever done? What I wanted was to be able to answer *that* question.

Chapter Seven

An injustice of fifth grade was the restricted recess. We now can only go on the playground before school (if you're lucky enough to be one of those with earlier bus routes) and for twenty minutes after lunch. That was it. Twenty minutes! Which really stunk if every one of your friends—all four of them—were in different classes or, in April's case, a different school. Even worse, our part of the playground was about to be under construction.

Our playground had two parts—a fancy new playscape with tunnel slides and a tower, and the old playground, with metal monkey bars and rusting swings. But the thing is, the new playscape was quickly claimed by jerkface Tom and all of his minions, leaving the rest of us to hang out in the older section. It's fine, though. I mean, racing down the tunnels with friends probably was only fun the first dozen or so times. It wasn't worth dealing with them and their tendency to accidentally-on-purpose push people down the slides before they were ready or block the ladders to the top.

Mom complained a lot about the PTO's endless fund-raising to tear down the old playground and replace it with another fancy new one. A couple of times over the summer, Mom brought Molly and me to the school to play on the playground, and she'd sigh and roll her eyes at how the old playground was sectioned off with yellow tape because the PTO was surveying it. Now that school's back in session, the yellow tape is gone and we're allowed back onto it. Jerkface Tom and his buddies kept coming over to the old section, chasing one another and hooting like they were raiding a village or something.

I just knew when the PTO replaced the old section, Tom and his friends were going to claim it, but at least the pack and I would have the now-old section.

When the lunch bell rang the next day, everyone rushed out to the playground in a huge wave. Friday at last! Last year, our pack always headed straight for the top of the old monkey bars, but now we were scouting out a new location. Mostly it was because no one wanted to see Sam try and climb to the top with his huge cast, but also because the beginning of the school year tended to shake up who went where and when.

We weren't alone in scouting out new hangout space or vacating old spots. Take, for example, Lily. She used to be part of a trio of girls all with L names that end in y —Lily, Lainey, and Livy. Last year, before I had my pack, I had considered picking up a jump rope and hanging out by the hopscotch area where they always skipped— my name was a perfect invite, right?—but whenever I lurked by them, they drifted away. I now understood why. Lily thought I was named Lisa. I was sure that was the explanation.

New this year was the football group, which took over the open field behind the old and new playscapes. But I wasn't sure how much of a group they really were since teachers broke them up about ten minutes into recess for ramming into each other.

My pack had decided we would try the old swing set this year. The swings themselves were super low, so that the mulch around them was shoved back like a big bowl and the ground itself was dirt packed from kids dragging their feet back and forth. I got there first and sat right in the middle, grabbing the chain for the swings on either side and waiting for my pack to show up. Finally Shemanda arrived. "Where's Sam?" I asked peeking over their shoulders.

"A bunch of kids asked to sign his cast on the way out of school," Sheldon said. He grabbed one of the chains from me.

Amanda settled on the other side. I suddenly felt like a slippery piece of ham in a sandwich as the two of them timed their swings so they'd be behind or in front of me at the same time.

"What's that?" Sheldon suddenly gasped, and plopped straight off the swing. Without getting up, he army crawled forward.

Beside me, Amanda slipped off her swing, too. "One o'clock," she whispered and dropped to her belly.

"No, it isn't," I said. "It's barely twelve-fifty. We have ten more minutes of recess."

But Shemanda ignored me, turning in unison slightly to the right. They shimmied forward on the mulch. "There!" Sheldon suddenly yelped.

Out from the mulch suddenly popped a foot. For real! Not a human foot, thankfully. A teeny, tiny green and scale-covered foot. Then a second foot. And finally a narrow, dark head the size of an almond with black bead eyes and bright reddish-orange neck. Amanda stretched her fingers toward it, to push the mulch away. "No!" Sheldon barked. "It has to do it on its own."

"What is it?" I asked, finally stalling on the swing. Should I drop down, too? I glanced around; no one else seemed to have noticed what was happening. I tiptoed over to them just in case there were more of whatever it was underfoot.

"A baby turtle!" Sheldon gushed as it finally pushed itself to the surface. He squinted at the turtle, and pointed at its teeny shell with a shaking finger. "It's a wood turtle," he whispered. "They're seriously in danger. Only a few of them left. Oh-em-gee! Oh-em-gee!"

"Look!" Amanda pointed to another stirring mound of mulch. Around us was a third, fourth, fifth walnut-sized turtle emerging from the mulch.

"What's going on?" someone asked. Kids were starting to crowd around.

Sheldon hopped to his feet in one fluid motion. For a dorky kid, he had mad muscle control. "Back off! Back off!"

Beside me, Amanda muttered, "Uh-oh."

I winced when someone else stepped forward and Sheldon's neck veins popped to the surface. He bellowed, "Everyone, off the playscape! *Now!* This is a turtle hot zone!"

His eyes widened as everyone actually listened, taking a giant backward step en masse. He probably didn't realize that Amanda lurked just behind him, her arms crossed and scowl wide. I had seen this go down before—back in camp when Sheldon and Amanda unearthed a fossil.

"They could be anywhere!" Sheldon sent darting looks around the mulch and moved up onto his tiptoes. Amanda didn't. I'm not sure she could. But she did carefully step toward the edge of the playscape. "Mother turtles lay about a dozen eggs but only six crawled out of the mulch. The rest could hibernate here all winter. Oh-em-gee! Oh-em-gee!"

"Kumbaya." Amanda took a deep, noisy breath through her nose and out her mouth. "*Kumbaya!*" she screeched right in a kid's face as he stretched to see around her.

"So we're just supposed to stand on the basketball court?" someone whined as Shemanda herded people onto the blacktop. Sensing stuff was going down, tons of kids rushed toward us. Soon they spilled off the blacktop to the field, and now the football players were yelling about their game being interrupted.

"Yes!" Shemanda said together. Growled, really.

"Hey!" That jerkface Tom elbowed his way to the front. "We're playing tag. Get out of the way."

Sheldon held out his skinny arms and stretched apart his legs like he was a human wall. "Not on my watch. Not today."

"What's going on?" Miss Parker moved to the line of students circling the playscape.

"Baby turtles are hatching," Sheldon practically screeched. "We need to clear the playscape! They could get trampled!" As he said it, a sixth turtle scurried up and over Sheldon's dino sneakers. "Gah! Back up! Back up!"

Everyone took another collective step backward.

"What else do they need?" Miss Parker asked.

Sheldon blinked at Miss Parker. I think he wasn't used to having someone—especially a teacher—talk to him as if he had a real opinion worth listening to. "Um, we need to not help them. Crawling up and out of the mulch helps them get strong enough to leave this area, probably for a stream in the woods."

"How long will this take?" Tom groaned.

Miss Parker didn't answer, just nodded toward Sheldon to continue. "Um," he said, looking around. "Well, there are only a few hatched now. Another six or so could still be buried."

"So they'll need a couple days, three or four, to hatch?" Miss Parker asked.

"Three to four days?" Tom echoed in disgust. All around us, kids started groaning. Sure, a few were crouched down watching the little baby turtles scamper off the playscape toward the woods behind the school, but most were trying to outdo who could show Tom they were just as mad. "No way we're going to skip running around at recess for three or four days just because of some stupid turtles."

"No, it's going to take a lot longer." Sheldon shook his head. "The others could be hibernating in their nest. They could stay there until spring."

Miss Parker tilted her head. "How do you know this?" she asked, but not in a what-do-you-know questioning way, more like she was curious.

Sheldon's cheeks flushed. "Turtles are in the archelosauria family. Their closest relatives are dinosaurs."

"And birds," Amanda cut in. "That's what you always tell me."

"That's right," Sheldon said. Shemanda smiled and had a little moment.

"Sheldon knows everything there is to know about dinosaurs. And apparently turtles, too," I told Miss Parker. "If he says there are more baby turtles buried, he's right."

"Hmm." Miss Parker's eyes scanned the mulch.

"What's it matter? They're going to bulldoze this whole playground in a month." Tom snorted.

Sheldon's face turned scary white. He was either going to explode or collapse. Quickly I put my hand on his shoulder and squeezed. To Tom, I said, "We're not going to let that happen."

"It's not up to you," Tom snarled. "My mom's on the PTO. She says they're going to start building in two months."

I crossed my arms. "This is a restricted area! Zoned for conservation!"

Miss Parker tilted her head. "I'm not sure you have the authority to do that." She smiled. "Yet." Then she turned toward the cluster of kids around and behind her. "We'll discuss this later, but right now it's time to go in." She blew the whistle hanging around her neck.

"We still have five more minutes!" Tom groaned. Okay, here's the truth. *I* said that. But after it came out of my mouth, I realized it was a Tom thing to say, so let's just pretend he was the one who said it.

Miss Parker blew her whistle again. I tiptoed off the mulch to the blacktop and then stomped inside. Shemanda were the last ones one in, busy guarding the baby turtle pit, but I was the second to last. Just in front of me was that jerkface Tom, stomping just like I was (until I saw him doing it, and then I just walked).

I didn't realize until the doors clicked closed behind me that Sam never even came over to us during recess.

❖ ❖ ❖

"This year," Miss Parker said toward the end of social studies class, "we're going to focus a lot on the democratic process. One way we're illustrating that is through the upcoming school elections."

"Tom for president!" Henry, Tom's sidekick since forever, shouted out.

Tom stood and bowed. "I accept your nomination." He held out his hand to shake Henry's. "And I'd like to announce my running mate!" He hoisted Henry's hand in the air.

I didn't realize the barfing sounds were coming from me until Miss Parker cleared her throat and wrote my name on the whiteboard. That's a warning. Miss Parker said if she had to underline a person's name, that meant they had to miss five minutes of recess. If she circled the underlined name for a third offense, that meant a call home. I put my head down on the desk to keep my face from getting me into more trouble.

"*Anyone* interested in running for office may fill out the form and return it to a teacher." She pointed to the stack of papers at the corner of her desk. "They're due by the end of the day."

Miss Parker glanced around the classroom. "Whoever wins the nomination will get to add their voice to a number of issues facing our school."

"Like what?" Lily asked.

"Well, the fifth, sixth, and seventh grade presidents and vice presidents attend some PTO and school board meetings to represent their class. They weigh in on things like the homework policy and dress codes. The officers also convene together on school-wide ideas, such as fund-raisers and dances." Miss Parker smiled at the murmur that went through the room. "Each class president will run a platform—or set of ideas—and then work all year to make sure those goals are met and their classmates benefit."

I hoped whoever won would make refried beans a daily staple in the cafeteria and ban dodgeball forever.

Miss Parker continued, "The president and vice president would work with the PTO to weigh in on how their budget would best be spent. It's an important job.

"One way we vet, or decide whether we're going to support, candidates is by listening to them share and then debate their platforms. I thought it'd be fun if we had a class debate."

"On what?" Lily asked.

"Well, let's decide. What do you think we should debate?"

"How about how dumb it is to close down our playground for stupid turtles?" Tom smirked at me when I peeked up from my arm cave. He had no room in his jerk heart for anything, even turtles.

Miss Parker's marker squeaked against the whiteboard. Now I was the one to smirk. Jerkface Tom was getting his name on the board, too. Only Miss Parker's marker kept on squeaking, way longer than it took to write a three-letter name. I looked up. Across the board, she had written: *Should the playground close because of the turtles?*

"Yes, of course it should," I blurted. "They'll die if it doesn't. They're babies."

I waited for Miss Parker to underline my name for not raising my hand, but she just capped the marker and put it back on the tray. "Go ahead and grab your computers," she said. Fifth graders got to have little laptops in their classroom instead of going to computer lab like baby fourth graders. As everyone moved toward the laptop cart, she continued louder, "Spend the next ten minutes researching this topic. Decide which side you're on. I'm going to pass out index cards. On the lined side, write your notes to support your argument. On the blank side, in large letters write *pro* or *con*. Pro will mean you're in favor of closing down the playground and delaying construction because of the turtles. Con will mean you're against shutting down the playground renovation and want to proceed with construction."

Easy, right? Who could be anti-turtle?

Turns out, lots of people. That's who.

Chapter Eight

After our ten minutes, Miss Parker asked everyone to put away the laptops. She sat crisscross applesauce in the middle of her desk and asked us what we found out. Truth was, Sheldon was on to something with his turtle obsession. They were crazy interesting.

"Okay," Miss Parker said, after laying out the rules for the debate: only one person could speak at a time, we had to stick only to the turtle-playground issue, we had to stay calm and in control, and speakers had no more than two minutes to share their viewpoint. "Raise your index cards to show whether you're pro or con."

I held mine up over my head and looked around. Lollipop farts! Only two other people were pro. "Lily," I hissed, when I noticed her erasing her pro and scribbling con. "What are you doing?"

Lily shrugged. "Sorry, Lisa. The turtles will just need to find somewhere else to live."

"*Lucy*. They can't find somewhere else to live. They're *hibernating*!"

She shrugged again and held up her revised card.

"Okay." Miss Parker nodded around the room. "Who wants to speak first?"

Tom stood beside his desk. "We should have full access to all parts of our playground. It's not our fault a turtle popped out some eggs where we play. It's our playground." He turned toward the class, bolstering his arms like he was rallying the crowd at a soccer game. "It's our playground! It's our playground! It's our playground!" Sure enough, everyone joined in his chant, even as Miss Parker clapped her hands for them to stop.

I popped to my feet. "You don't even go on that part of the playground. Why do you care?"

A few people groaned and Tom rolled his eyes as he took his seat again.

"Stick to the issue, Lucy," Miss Parker reminded me. "What about Tom's point that the turtle made a poor choice in where to choose its habitat?"

I took a deep breath and thought about Sheldon. What would he say? For a moment, my mind warped him into a turtle, his skinny neck stretching up to his round head and his body a giant shell. I checked the notes I had made on the back of my card, but they were all blurry. "Um . . ." Tom snorted. I cleared my throat.

Miss Parker got up from her desk and stood in front of me. "Why do turtles need protection?"

"There aren't many of them left," I said, suddenly remembering my research. "Especially the wood turtle. That's the kind on the playground. There aren't many of them anymore because we keep taking their regular land and doing stupid stuff with it, like building playgrounds. They were here first, not us! We're bigger and we've got more power. We should take care of them."

"With great power comes great responsibility." Miss Parker smiled and patted my shoulder. I sat back down.

Tom popped back up. "So now our playground's stupid, huh? I suppose if all you've got are two friends—"

"Four!" I shouted at the same time that Miss Parker said, "Stop it!"

She strode over to Tom. "We will not make this personal and we will not attack our opponents, just the issue. Another outburst like that and you will no longer be able to participate."

Tom's ears turned red. Behind Miss Parker, I smiled at him wide and toothy to let him know how much I enjoyed seeing him get into trouble. "Okay, then." I quickly wiped the smile off my face as Miss Parker turned back toward me. "Lucy, would you like to raise another argument?"

"Yes." I stood. "We have other places to hang out at recess. We have other things we can do. These turtles will die if we don't protect them. Die! Isn't protecting their lives more important than a couple of dumb swings and a set of monkey bars?"

"Hmm," I heard a kid who sits two seats behind me murmur. "I don't want them to *die*." Lily scratched out con and wrote pro on her index card. Someone in the next row did, too.

Tom was on his feet before Miss Parker could even turn to him. "My mom's on the PTO. I saw the plans for that playground. They're awesome! An obstacle course. A zip line. A climbing wall!"

"Wow!" Lily blurted. "I love climbing walls!"

"Everyone loves climbing walls!" Tom repeated. "The point is, *maybe* there are more turtles hiding in the mulch. *Maybe*. But we don't know for sure. Why should our parents' hard work to raise money for a playground, why should our *right* to have fun at recess and run around be pushed aside for a couple of *maybe* turtles?"

As everyone around me clapped, I felt something horrible happen. The skin around my eyes burned. The people in front of me blurred. Oh, no. *Ohno-ohno-ohno.* I was going to cry. Cry like a baby in front of all of these people over a couple of turtles. I shook my head and squeezed shut my traitor eyes, forcing the tears to stay put. For a second, that image of shelled Sheldon popped back into my mind.

"Yes, we should," I said, and my voice was so strong, so powerful, it echoed around the room, bouncing off the walls and the superhero posters like a bell. Only it was the actual bell. Class was over. Over the clamor of kids packing up and grabbing their books, I yelled, "We should protect anyone who needs it. Anyone!"

I glanced around. A couple of the kids were nodding in my direction. Maybe I had convinced a few. I bet more agreed with me but just didn't want to show it with Tom and his crew watching. But it didn't matter much since the debate was over. Some were already headed toward the door.

"Hold on!" Miss Parker yelled. She held up her hand. Immediately, everyone stayed in place. "Just for a few seconds!" Miss Parker turned toward me. "Now remember, this is just a debate. We don't have the authority to make these discussions. But imagine if we did. Lucy, what if we held off construction until next summer? Is that a compromise we could all agree upon? Give the turtles the winter to hibernate and then resume construction?"

I wanted to say yes. But I couldn't. And when Tom shifted so I could see him out of the corner of my eye, a huge toothy smile plastered on his jerk face, I knew he knew it, too. He had found the same detail in his turtle research. "No," I said, feeling my eyes stinging all over again. "The mama turtle will come back in the summer to lay her eggs in the same spot. Every year, she'll lay her eggs there. We can never have the playground there."

Miss Parker sucked in her lips. I could tell she had been expecting a different response.

"Never?" Lily asked. "Sorry, turtles, but it's our playground." She crossed out pro and wrote con again.

"It's our playground!" Tom chanted as he marched out the door. Of course, most of the kids joined in. They kept the call going down the hall, even as I heard Mrs. Fredericks yelling at them to be quiet as they passed her library. "It's our playground! It's our playground!"

I don't know why—I mean, they're just turtles—but my eyes were stinging so hard then that I didn't even try not to cry. "Lucy," Miss Parker said. Her voice was quiet, not at all like the one she had used to make everyone turn to statues a moment earlier, but just as impossible to ignore.

I shoved my notebook into my backpack and didn't look up at her. I wiped at my scalded cheeks. "What?"

"Lucy," she said again. She sighed and sat down in Lily's empty seat right in front of me. "Lucy, have you considered running for student government?"

I caught myself just before uttering one of Tom's snorts. "I just lost that debate. By a lot." I did look up at her now, to see if she was making fun of me. She wasn't, I thought. She just smiled and looked me square in the eyes.

Miss Parker nodded. "Yes, you did. But what impresses me is that you didn't back down. You saw, I'm sure, a couple people turned their vote to con when they saw how the majority in the class fell."

"Thanks to Tom," I muttered.

"Tom's a strong leader," Miss Parker agreed. "But I think you could be, too. I think part of being a leader is sticking to what you believe, even when the odds are stacked against you. And you did that. You used facts and passion to make your point."

"It doesn't matter," I pointed out. "It's not like I got anyone to my side."

Miss Parker tilted her head. "Maybe not during this class. But I think you've given a lot of kids something to consider. Even though you didn't win the debate, you might've inspired a few people to stand up for what they believe, too."

Miss Parker's high heels clicked across the tiled floor as she strode over to the desk to grab a piece of paper. She held it out to me.

"Application for Student Government Position," I read aloud.

"It's due by the end of the day. Give it thought," Miss Parker said. "Being class president would be pretty awesome."

"Awesome?" I repeated. "I've been looking for my awesome."

Miss Parker's forehead wrinkled a little, but then she smiled, and the sunlight in the room made her teeth do that glinting thing again. "And it's also a pretty brave thing to do."

I smoothed the paper on the desk and picked up a pencil. Maybe she was right. Maybe this was my awesome. Maybe this was my brave thing. "This has a space for vice president, too."

Miss Parker nodded. "Most candidates run together, vice president and president." She stood as students trickled in for the next class. "The best strategy seems to be choosing someone with whom you work well, who has a similar viewpoint, but maybe brings something else to the table."

I bit my lip. "Like a beta wolf in a pack."

Miss Parker blinked at me. "You know a lot about animals, don't you?"

I shrugged, trying to be humble. Truth is, I know *everything* about wolves, just like Sam.

We were the leaders of our pack, just like the pack we met at the Able Wolf Sanctuary. Sam and I visited the sanctuary last year and saw the alpha Sascha. We were there when she joined forces with the beta wolf, Ralph. In our pack, I'm the alpha, and Sam's my Ralph. *Class President Lucy Beaner. Vice President Sam Righter*. I handed Miss Parker the filled-out form on the way out of the room.

"Are you sure?" Miss Parker glanced at the paper. "Does Mr. Righter know about this?"

"Of course!" I said. Or, at least, he'd *soon* know about this. Because this was going to be awesome! Even better, it was going to be our awesome.

"I had a suspicion you might've given this prior

consideration. Ms. Drake mentioned your leadership skills when we talked about my class this year." Miss Parker stood and held out her hand to shake mine. "Congratulations on your candidacy. We'll announce the running teams over the afternoon announcements on Monday. I'm going in alphabetical order for the super-lative chart, and since Megan Adams is out with the flu, you were going to be our first profiled student, with your poster due Monday. But I think it might be better to wait until after the elections since it seems I'll have two can-didates in the class—you and Tom—and I don't want to show favoritism."

She sighed. "I hope you're not disappointed at hav-ing to wait."

We both looked over at the current superlative list, with its blank space after "the bravest thing I've done is . . ."

"I'll get over it, Miss Parker."

❖ ❖ ❖

I finally caught up with Sam in the bus line at the end of the day. Sheldon was with him, since they ride the same bus. Mine was two down, with Amanda's in between, so I technically wasn't supposed to stop and talk but I had to let Sam know I found our awesome! I tried to ignore how every time I passed kids from my class, they chanted, "It's our playground!" Despite that, I could hear Sheldon going on and on about the "turtle hot zone" and not noticing that Sam was leaning against the wall and looking straight down at the tiles. I could guess why he was upset: if he hadn't broken his arm, he would've been at the gym right now, practicing.

Behind them, two girls were whispering to each other and pointing at Sam. They smiled and waved when he met their eyes and now his cheeks were bright red. My arms got all tingly and legs kicky at the sight. It'd been more than a week and people were still clustered around Sam like he was a YouTube star instead of just letting my friend be my friend. Who did they think they were?

"Can I sign your cast?" One of the girls sidled up to Sam, her cheeks pink and smile wide enough to catch flies.

"Didn't you already sign it an hour ago?" Sam twisted his arm a little to check for her signature.

"But I could do it again," the girl said. "I saw you in the newspaper last night. I liked the picture of you. You're so—"

"I'm sorry," Sam interrupted, "I'm talking with Sheldon." He turned so his back was to the girl.

"But—" the girl whined.

"Listen," I interrupted her, pulling on my best presidential face (an expression that shows both concern and compassion while also maintaining dignity). "Sam will allow cast signings at the beginning of recess and the end of lunch. Other than that, he needs to concentrate on his recuper . . . recupa . . . on getting better."

"What's wrong with your face?" Sam whispered.

"What makes you Sam's spokesperson?" The girl glared at me.

"Lucy's my best friend," Sam said. "And it, um, hurts to have my arm knocked around a lot. So just like Lucy said, I've got to, um, recupcrate."

The girl nodded and then pranced back to her friend, who said, "I can't believe you were going to tell him he's so cute! You're so brave!" The two giggled and I threw up in my mouth. Second time today. But then I remembered: these were voters. I plastered on another presidential smile. Both girls scrunched up their noses like my smile was stinky and fell into familiar, hissing whispers. And you know what? I wasn't even mad. They didn't have to like me. They just had to vote for me.

Thanks to hero Sam as my VP, that's just what they'd do.

"Sam." I nudged him. "I need to talk to you!"

"I'll tell you more later, man," Sheldon said and called out to Amanda in the next line. "Let's have a Shelled One meeting at four o'clock. My house!"

"Shelled One?" I asked, distracted.

"Yeah, that's what we're calling the call to action. Save the Shelled Ones!" Sheldon raised his skinny fist.

"And the fact that it sounds a lot like Sheldon is just a coincidence?"

Sheldon grinned. "So are you in?"

"In on what?"

"The Save the Shelled Ones Campaign meeting at my house this afternoon."

"I'm not sure I can make it." It's grocery night, and if I went with Dad, we'd be coming home with rotisserie chicken, deli-made mac and cheese, and peach cobbler. I licked my lips just thinking about it. Saving turtles—and hanging out with my pack—is important, but a girl's got to eat while the eating's good.

"It's only the first campaign meeting," Sheldon said. "You can come to the next one."

Speaking of campaigns . . . I turned back to Sam.

Time to tell him the exciting news! Only his face was a lot grouchier than a vice president's should probably be. Maybe I would have to ease him into this. "Where've you been all day?"

Sam shrugged. He stared back down at his shoes some more. It was like an invisible weighted blanket draped over him, pushing down his shoulders, slumping him back, and even making his knees dip a little.

"Is your arm bothering you?"

Sam rolled his eyes. "Does it matter?"

"What's that supposed to mean?"

Sam met my eyes and for some reason they started to sting again. I wasn't used to seeing my friend so angry. "Even if my arm felt great, it wouldn't matter. I'm off the team." He leaned against the wall again. I did, too, just next to him.

"When your arm's better, you're going to catch right back up." I bumped into his good side. "Until then, maybe you could find something else to focus on?" Like running for vice president . . .

Sam knocked the back of his head against the wall. "No, I won't catch up. I had an appointment with my doctor last night. My coach came, too, I thought to be supportive. But really it was just to find out the deets.

The break I have, it's not going to heal so that it's the same as before. I'll never get back to where I was. Not even close. I'm done."

"You can't know that," I whispered.

"So you think you know more than my doctor now?" Sam's voice was cold. Without even thinking about it, I inched away from him. "I'm sorry," he said and suddenly sounded like my Sam again. "I'm sorry. I just—" He took a deep breath as I fell back against the wall where I had been. "I was supposed to compete this weekend at a meet. A big one. And now . . . ."

"Well, as it turns out," I said and clapped my hands. "My plans fell through for this weekend, too."

"What were your plans?" Sam asked.

"Netflix." I shrugged. "Mom changed the Wi-Fi password and won't tell me what it is until I clean my room. But she didn't necessarily tell me I *had* to clean my room so I'm just going to see how long I can live off cable."

"I don't know, Lucy. I don't feel much like doing anything. I'm not myself. I'm . . . ."

"Incredibly grouchy and not all that nice," I pointed out. "But that's okay. You kind of deserve to feel that way."

Sam ground his teeth together. "I'm sorry," he muttered.

"No biggie. Anyway," I continued, "I don't have plans, either. So let's do something fun!" Like work on campaign speeches, I thought. But I figured now was not to the time to tell Sam I had stumbled upon our awesome. He needed to be a little cheerier. A little more hopeful. A little less like a hibernating turtle. "That's it!"

"What's it?" Sam squinted even more.

"Able Wolf Sanctuary!" I bounced on my toes. "We haven't been there in forever. Let's go check on Ralph and Sascha. My dad's been saying he really wants to check out the sanctuary. I bet he'll take us."

"I don't know." The bus monitor blew her whistle and Sam trudged forward toward his bus, pushing his backpack up on his good shoulder.

"Come on!" I said. "It'll be fun. What else are you going to do? Spend all weekend being sad?"

"Maybe." Sam turned back to me and for just a second, I saw the flash of his dimple.

I laughed. "Come on!"

"Okay," he said. "Let's go."

"Aaarrroooo!" I howled just to make him laugh. It worked. I stayed put, even as Sam took his seat on the bus. He sat down and threw back his head like he was howling, too. I knew he was just acting like he was howling, not actually making a sound. But I grinned anyway, so happy that he lost some of his sadness.

I'd wait to tell him he was going to be my vice president when we were at the sanctuary. Maybe when he saw how awesome Ralph and Sascha were, *he* would suggest teaming up. And I could be like, *I already took care of the form*. And he'd be like, *Lucy, you're amazing*. And he'd stare at me with those chocolate-brown eyes and I'd stare back and then . . . Scratch that. That went in a weird direction. He'd fist-bump me and we'd howl. That's how it'd end. Even though I could see my bus line two rows down was loading onto the bus, I took a moment to howl again. "Aaaaarrrrooo!"

"Loser!" Tom shouted from his bus line.

Whatever. He'd see the real loser soon enough. On election day.

Chapter Nine

"Dad, we need to go!" I stood by the door, hand on the handle, waiting for my pokey-pants dad to fill up a travel mug with coffee so we could hit the road for Able Wolf Sanctuary. First stop, of course, was Sam's house. "Go, go, go!"

Dad screwed the lid on his mug and scratched the back of his head. "Lucy, the wolves aren't going anywhere. They're in pens."

"Enclosures," I corrected. "And the enclosures are huge, so you can't always even see the wolves."

Finally Dad shrugged on his coat. "Let's go," he said around the granola bar he had shoved in his mouth. I whipped open the door.

Mom walked sleepily down the hall in her robe,

Molly on her hip. "Hold up!" she said, and looked down at the phone in her hand. "I just got a text from Sam's mom. He's not feeling up to going today."

"No!" I pulled the door shut again. "Why?"

Mom shook her head. "She doesn't say. Maybe something to do with his arm?"

"But this whole trip was for him! Now how am I going to show him he's a leader and needs to run for class vice president?"

Mom and Dad both turned on me with narrowed eyes. Even Molly lifted her head from Mom's shoulder to stare my way. "Lucy," Mom said sharply. "Are you trying to manipulate your friend?"

"Again?" Dad tacked on.

I crossed my arms. "I'm not manipulating. I just was going to wait until we're in the right setting and then suggest an idea that I think would be really, really good for Sam."

"*Vice* president?" Mom tilted her head. "And president would be . . ."

My face suddenly caught fire on the inside. "Me."

Dad smiled. "My daughter. Madame President."

Mom laughed. "And already thinking like a politician." She shifted Molly to her other hip. "If you want to be president, that's wonderful, Lucy. But it's not okay to set up your friends or play with their emotions to get what you want."

"That's not what I'm doing!" I gasped. "I think he'd do a great job."

"I'm sure he would," Mom agreed. Molly seemed to also, shaking a fist in the air. Of course, then she shoved the fist into her mouth and drooled all over it, so maybe she wasn't really cheering for Sam. "But that's his decision. Not yours."

I sucked on my lip.

"What did you do, Lucy?" Dad groaned.

"The forms were due yesterday and so I—"

"You didn't," Mom gasped. Molly definitely was shaking her spitty fist at me now.

"It was an accident," I mumbled.

"You have to tell Sam. From everything you've told me, he hates the spotlight. Do you really think he's going to want to run for vice president?"

"Maybe."

Dad pulled Molly from Mom's arms to blow kisses on her cheek. When she giggled, he squeezed her and handed her back to Mom before turning to me. "You're going to have to tell him. Today."

"Fine," I said, "but can we go to the sanctuary anyway?"

Dad twirled his keys on his finger. "Yes, but—"

"I'll tell him! I'll tell him!"

✧ ✧ ✧

April's aunt Shelley, who works at the sanctuary, parked her golf cart at the boundary of Sascha and Ralph's enclosure.

"These are the two that remind you of you and Sam?" asked Dad, watching as Ralph chased Sascha around a giant boulder in the middle. He laughed.

"What?" I asked.

"Just, looks about right," he answered as the wolves changed course and now Sascha was chasing Ralph. "Why isn't he the alpha?" Dad asked Aunt Shelley. "I mean, he's a lot bigger than her. I thought the biggest wolves were always the alphas."

Wow, Dad was right! Ralph was bigger than Sascha now. He had grown a few inches taller and even wider. A strip of skin around his neck still was bare from the horrible collar he had been forced to wear, but I couldn't see his ribs anymore and his coat was glossier.

Aunt Shelley laughed. It sounded like pebbles being shaken in a paper bag. She put her foot up on the edge of the golf cart, crossed her thick, tan arms, and smiled into her fist. "Size don't matter none to these two."

"But isn't the goal to be alpha?" Dad pressed. "I mean, isn't that what every wolf wants?"

Aunt Shelley shook her head. She barely ever spoke, and when she did, I found myself leaning in to catch her tumbling, gruff words. "Some wolves, like Ralph here, just want to belong. That's all. Just wanna know they belong to someone."

❖ ❖ ❖

Monday morning, I waited for Sam by his bus line. Yes, I had thought a lot about just calling Sam over the weekend and letting him know he was going to be my vice president (and maybe that's even exactly what I told Mom and Dad I had done), but then I told myself how much better it would be to give him this exciting news in person. I'm very good at talking myself out of doing stuff.

But no more stalling. Ms. Drake was going to announce the candidates over the loudspeaker before the end of the day, so I had to tell him.

"Give it up," Becky huffed just behind me. She crossed her arms and rolled her eyes. "He doesn't like you. He doesn't like anybody, he told me."

"What are you talking about?" I half turned around, still keeping my eye on the approaching bus. I didn't see Sam in his usual seat, but that didn't mean anything. He could've been sitting with Sheldon or slouched down low.

"Sam." Becky uncrossed her arms to point to the bus and rolled her eyes again.

"Sam does so like me. I'm his best friend." I rolled my eyes, too. Have you ever noticed how contagious eye rolling is? It's worse than a yawn.

"But he doesn't *like you* like you," Becky said. "He told me he doesn't like anyone."

The bus doors opened and out spilled all of the kids. Everyone but Sam. Where was he? Oh, lollipop farts! Sheldon was the last one off the bus. I grabbed him by the T-shirt with two hands. "Where is Sam?"

"Calm down, Lucy." Sheldon backed up and smoothed the wrinkles I had made at the shoulders of his shirt. "This shirt is vintage." I stepped back to look at it. Of course it was a dinosaur, a T-Rex trying to make its bed with little tiny arms. "Funny, isn't it? It's from the nineties."

No time for laughter, now that my day was about to nose-dive into oh-no-what-did-I-do-now. "Where's Sam?" I asked again.

Sheldon smiled. "No worries, Lucy. He's coming to school late, after a doctor's appointment to check his arm. He's going to be here for the big announcement later this afternoon."

"What announcement?" I asked, stepping backward.

"That he's a candidate." Sheldon tilted his head. "Obviously."

"Obviously," I echoed. Wait. What? How had Sam found out? Maybe Ms. Drake told him? Or Miss Parker? Or . . . maybe *I* had told him? Maybe I let it slip and hadn't even realized it. Slowly, like water let out of the bathtub, I felt all of my worry and stress just circle and drain, circle and drain. Sam already knew! And, given that he had told Sheldon about it and that he'd be back in time for the announcement, that meant *he was okay with it.*

"That's great!" I chirped. "Sheldon, that's amazing!"

"I know, right?" Sheldon nodded. He was super smiley today. He nodded to a few guys passing by on the other side. A couple nodded back and then looked around to make sure no one had seen. A few more just looked behind them like they wondered who Sheldon could be greeting. "We're going to put up signs after school if you want to help."

"Wow!" I stepped back. And now I wasn't just drained from worry, I was floating with happiness. My pack totally had my back. Of course they were on board. They were even making signs for me! "That's so cool."

Sheldon shrugged. "I know we haven't had a lot of time to talk, Lucy, but I've got so many ideas—"

The bell rang, slicing through the air and reminding me that I had to get my floating self to the other side of the building. "I can't wait to hear them," I gushed, shuffling backward from Sheldon toward the doors. "I'm going to represent you well! The whole school well!"

Sheldon's wide smile fell a little at that—I guessed he really had wanted a chance to talk about the Shelled Ones (little did he know I already voiced my support for the cause!). I sprinted to Miss Parker's room. This was going to be the best day ever!

(Do me a favor. If I ever say that again, just kick me the shins or knock me over or shave off one of my eyebrows. Crush my heart into your fist and then stomp on it. Get it over with.)

❖ ❖ ❖

Best day ever.

What a joke.

I can't quite pinpoint when I realized everything was going wrong, but I started to get glimmers at lunch. No one was at my table. My whole pack was gone, and I was once more a solo eater. Even worse: it was turkey ham day. Not a refried bean in sight.

Of course all of that would change once I was president. Not just the delegation of turkey ham to only one day a month and the institution of refried beans as a daily option, but also an end to the solo eating.

Sam and I would probably have to put Amanda in charge of keeping throngs of students at bay while we enjoyed our meals. They'd want to discuss their concerns or take selfies with us or present us with ideas only we could fix. We'd have to politely remind them that such things needed to wait. There's a time and a place, people. "Please make an appointment with the class secretary," Sheldon, our campaign manager, would tell them.

I'm not sure what the class secretary did exactly, but that was another position that students could run for in the election, along with treasurer and historian. Miss Parker said that she'd give each candidate a manual detailing the officers' responsibilities and a breakdown of what other officers did once the candidates were announced. But I was guessing the secretary booked appointments for the president, the treasurer counted the money the president had to spend on school stuff, and the historian took notes on the president's accomplishments.

I kept my eyes on the door as I ate the edges of the turkey ham sandwich. Where was my pack? Sheldon and

Amanda were probably keeping an eye on the turtle nesting area from a window nearby. Miss Parker had told the class that morning that the old playground was roped off while the administration and PTO decided what to do about the turtles. Tom had groaned and slouched in his chair, but since it had been raining all day and we were going to have indoor recess anyway, I didn't see what the big deal was.

I hoped the pack would show up soon. We had to have indoor recess in our homerooms, which meant this was my only time to see them all day. The two girls who had been trying to sign Sam's cast again wandered by carrying their lunch trays, still giggly and whispery.

"He's *so* cute. Did you see his dimple?"

"Are you guys talking about Sam?" I stood up, blocking the girls from passing by.

"So what if we are?" they somehow said together.

"Because I need to find him," I said. I grabbed my tray, ready to dump it and go to wherever they said he was.

The two girls looked at each other. I noticed that though they looked nothing alike—one was tall and pale, with thick blonde hair lying flat down her back; the other was short and dark, with curly hair surrounding her pixie face—they somehow had the same face. The same reactions. The same look. Then one of them jutted out her hip and the other tilted her head. "Listen," hip jutter said, "if he wanted your help in the library, he would've asked for your help."

"Help? Library?"

"Great job, Stacey," the other girl said. "Now she knows he's in the library." She stomped off toward the table, the other following behind her apologizing. I watched them, my mouth hanging open for just a second. The way they followed each other, seemed to think the exact same way one moment, but were mean to each other the next—it was just like me and Becky a year earlier. Wow. Thankfully I had real friends now, ones that didn't care if you did your hair differently or liked someone they didn't or talked about things they didn't care about in the same way.

I emptied my tray and rushed toward the library, a grin stretching across my face when I saw them—my friends gathered around a table with Mrs. Fredericks standing just behind. She was handing them a bin of markers, not grouching at all even though Amanda was eating a sandwich right there in the library.

"Thanks!" Sam said, and I could hear the smile in his

voice even though his head was bent down on whatever he was working on.

I bounced and clapped as I got closer, because they were making posters! That's why they weren't at lunch. They were too busy surprising me with campaign posters!

"Hey, Lucy!" Sheldon stood up and skinny fist pumped the air. "You're here! Look, guys, Lucy's here, too!"

"Hey," Sam said without looking up. Amanda was trying to get the cap off a Sharpie but she sort of nodded my way.

Sheldon continued, "We realized we forgot to tell you where we were and felt so bad but the Gob—I mean, Mrs. Fredericks—said we couldn't be wandering the halls alone over lunch." He smiled at Mrs. Fredericks and in a higher-pitched voice said, "And she was so nice to let us use this space over lunch."

Turns out, Mrs. Frederick's face wasn't made of concrete that'd be sure to crumble if she ever smiled. Because that's just what she did then. She smiled. I gasped. Mrs. Fredericks never smiled. "Of course you may use this space. A hero like Sam is always welcome." She ruffled the top of Sam's head. "Did I tell you my grandbabies are twins, same age as the ones you saved?"

"Yeah," Sam said quietly. "You mentioned it."

"About a thousand times," Amanda muttered.

I stepped forward, working to keep my face flat so I could paint it surprised when I saw they were making me campaign posters. "So what are you guys working on?"

"Check it out!" Sheldon held up a huge poster. I didn't have to worry about faking a surprise face anymore.

The poster had an enormous hand-drawn turtle in the middle. SAVE THE SHELLED ONES was scrawled across the top in green. Across the bottom, in red capital letters, was the following: VOTE AUTUMN GROVE HERO SAM RIGHTER FOR PRESIDENT. Just below that, in green again: SHELDON HARRIS FOR VICE PRESIDENT.

Chapter Ten

I rushed from the library without saying a word to anyone in my pack.

"Lucy, wait," Sam called out. But I couldn't. How could they do this without telling me? I was their alpha!

Unless I wasn't.

I had to tell Miss Parker that I wasn't running for president anymore. I definitely had to stop Ms. Drake from announcing Sam as my running mate. And quick! But already there were six kids lined up in front of me to talk with her. This was how every class with her kicked off—a line of kids waiting to talk to her like she was a celebrity or something. And she smiled and chatted with each and every one of them. Which, I guess, is why we all waited to talk to her. I'd only done it a couple of times, like when I wanted her to know about Molly rolling over, about that time I climbed the pine tree in my backyard when I was six, and other important things like that.

Most of the kids in front of me didn't even have actual issues! Life or death issues! "Can I sneak in front of you?" I asked Lily.

"No." She didn't even turn around.

"But I *have* to talk to Miss Parker."

"We all do," Lily said.

"What do you have to tell her? My thing is time sensitive!" The afternoon announcements were at the end of this class. If I didn't get down to Ms. Drake's office before class, it might be too late to catch her before the afternoon announcements.

"Mine is, too," said Lily without turning around.

So I waited. And I waited. Tom had to tell Miss Parker that the soccer team was heading to the championship. A girl named Katie told her that she was going to Colorado in two weeks to visit her great-aunt Stella. Henry told her (again) about the same dumb soccer championship. (C'mon, people!) Allison McPatrick had to say that question sixteen on last week's grammar test could've been interpreted differently and did Miss Parker know that she was reading *Wuthering Heights*? (Yes! Yes! Miss Parker knows you're reading *Wuthering Heights*! Everyone knows you're reading *Wuthering Heights*. It's all you talk about, Allison McPatrick, even though you call it Withering instead of Wuthering, and I know for a fact that you're at my reading level and you totally skip lines when you read. No one turns pages that fast! No one!). "Yes, Allison," Miss Parker said in her super calm way. "That's pretty ambitious. I'm sure in a few years you'll have even more perspective on the story." Ugh! Hurry up, people! Pedro Chafetz just handed Miss Parker a note and went to his seat. Good man, that Pedro. Finally only Lily was ahead of me.

Lily leaned her hip against Miss Parker's desk. "You'll never guess what happened last night!"

"Hmm," Miss Parker said. "You found out that your fingers are actually toes?"

"No!" Lily giggled.

"You discovered a super power—maybe that you can fly but only when everyone else is asleep?"

"Uh-uh." Lily laughed again.

"Your little brother turned into a goldfish?"

"Silly Miss Parker! No, keep guessing!"

"You—"

I cleared my throat. Miss Parker's eyes slid toward me and back to Lily. "You tell me."

"I got a kitten!" Lily chirped.

"A kitten! What's his name?"

"Guess!" Lily said.

I wasn't long for this world. At any second, I'd burst into panic flames and flutter out the window in a cloud of Lucy smoke and everyone would be sorry then. I guessed a groan or plea for help leaked through my lips because Lily scowled over her shoulder at me. "Wait your turn!" she snapped.

"Time sensitive!" I hissed back.

"Oh, my." Miss Parker got up from the desk. "Look at the time! Lily, tell me more about the cat after class. Lucy, check in with me then, too."

"But—"

"Everyone, please take a seat!"

"But—"

"Lucy, whatever it is, it'll have to wait."

I stomped to my seat and slouched down in it. But not all hope was lost. If I sprinted straight to the office after this class, I'd be able to reach Ms. Drake before the announcements. She always began them just before buses arrived at three-twenty, after everyone had a chance to go to their lockers and pack up for the bus lines. I'd be fine. Everything was going to be just fine, I told myself. *We're going to be fine.*

"This afternoon," Miss Parker said, "we're going to hear about who intends to run for class officer positions.

These will be your class leaders, representing you to our PTO, the school board, and the administration. To help us realize the importance of great leadership, we're going to talk today about great American leaders through time and what has made them successful."

Did you know George Washington had a chance to be king? Miss Parker told us that it's a myth that the first president was offered the position of king of America, but she said since he was the first president, he could've pushed for more power, could've made it so he was *like* a king. But he didn't. He wanted instead to make sure that everything was as fair as possible. After all, he had stood up to a king! He didn't want to be one. And later, when the country was just a few years old, Washington faced a lot of protests and anger when he signed a treaty with Britain rather than go into another war. "He didn't do what was popular, but he did do what was right," Miss Parker pointed out.

Did you know Harriet Tubman escaped from slavery and then *went back* to rescue her mom? And then kept going back to rescue more and more people until the Union army just went ahead and made her a spy. A real spy! She was the first woman ever to lead an armed raid and saved seven hundred people. Seven hundred!

Did you know when Eleanor Roosevelt was First

Lady, women weren't allowed to vote and people with brown skin didn't have as many rights as people with white skin? Eleanor Roosevelt knew this was wrong and did what she could to change it, even though she got a ton of hate mail and a lot of people made fun of her. But she didn't just say it was wrong for people to be separated because of their skin, she did stuff to make it change. So in 1941, when some people thought black pilots couldn't do their job well, she didn't just argue about it. Instead, she jumped in the back of one of the pilot's planes and went for a ride. Pretty soon after that, black pilots were trained at Tuskegee Institute. Across the board, Miss Parker wrote this quote from Roosevelt: *We do not have to be heroes overnight. Just a step at a time, meeting each thing that comes up, seeing it not as dreadful as it appears, discovering that we have the strength to stare it down.*

"So," Miss Parker said, "what makes a strong leader?"

Lily raised her hand. "They're brave."

Miss Parker nodded. "Absolutely." She wrote *brave* under the quote. "What else?"

"They're not afraid to not be liked," I said before I realized the words were coming out of my mouth. Miss Parker wrote *self-confident* on the board.

"That won't be a problem for you," Tom muttered when Miss Parker's back was turned. I stuck my tongue out at him.

"Did you have something to add, Mr. Lemmings?" Miss Parker asked Tom.

"Yeah," he said kind of sudden. "Um, they're heroes."

Miss Parker added *hero*. "So who are some great leaders in your life?"

Tom raised his hand. "Well, I led the Autumn Grove Bearcats to the state soccer championships."

"Woot, woot!" Henry cheered.

Miss Parker crossed her arms but her voice stayed light and easy. "And how does that embody our standards—brave, self-confident and heroic?"

Tom leaned back in his chair, his legs stretching out in front of him and arms spread across the desk. He did that a lot, making himself take up a lot of space. Usually what followed confirmed his status as King Jerkface of the Kingdom Jerkface. "I'm brave because I pretty much could've won the game entirely on my own."

Henry's "woot" was a lot weaker after that.

But Tom wasn't done. "And I'm self-confident because I'm the best player on the team. And I'm heroic because I got the winning goal."

"And there we go." I rolled my eyes.

"Lucy?" Miss Parker turned back to me.

"Seriously? It's not brave to hog the ball. It's not being confident to say you're the best. That's being—" *King Jerkface from Kingdom Jerkface,* my thought maker supplied, but Miss Parker's "ahem" made me scramble for a different word. "That's being braggy. And it's not being a hero to win. That's just playing the game."

Tom shrugged. "What would you know? When you have won something or been brave or been a hero?"

Again my brain supplied a bunch of useless answers. Like that I was brave because once I read a scary book of Mom's about an evil clown and when I woke up in the middle of the night and remembered how scary it was, I threw it down the basement stairs even though it meant leaving my warm bed and walking down the hall alone—and, worst of all, opening the basement door, even though the darkness down the stairs was so thick and black it was like the giant pupil of an evil clown's eye staring back at me. And I wanted to tell him I had won stuff—in fact, I once won a free chicken potpie from the church raffle but it was full of slippery gravy and was frankly a disappointment (chicken and peas have no business calling themselves pie).

But a smarter part of my brain knew those weren't the kind of answers that would help me win this argument. So I told that part of my brain to think harder and told the still-grossed-out-about-the-gravy-soaked-peas part of my brain to move on to better thoughts, which I guess made for some really strange facial convulsions because when I opened my eyes everyone was staring at me.

"Lucy, are you okay?" Miss Parker asked.

"I'm a hero," the gravy-pea part of my brain took over and blurted. Tom snort-laughed and before Miss Parker could say anything the ping of the loudspeaker made everyone quiet except for every bit of my insides, which suddenly screeched like a dog whistle only I could hear. *Nonononononono! Don't be Ms. Drake! Nonononononono!*

"Excuse the interruption," Ms. Drake's voice called through the room. "I'm making our afternoon announcements early today due to the exciting nature of the information." She cleared her throat.

I jumped to my feet. "Miss Parker! I—go!" the words stumbled out. C'mon, thought maker! Get back in charge here! "I have to go," I tried again and bolted toward the door.

Miss Parker stood in front of it. "Back to your seat, Lucy." She dipped lower so she could whisper. "Don't be scared; this is exciting news."

"You don't understand," I whispered back. "I have to—"

But Ms. Drake's voice cut through us and Miss Parker pushed me back into the seat. "We have three candidates for our fifth-grade class president this year. These include Tom Lemming, with his vice presidential running mate of Henry Jacobson." Tom and Henry jumped to their feet and high-fived while the rest of the class (minus me) cheered. "Also running is Sam Righter as president with running mate Sheldon Harris."

Tom and Henry snort-laughed and rolled their eyes and my leg wanted to do all sorts of shin kicking. But I was too paralyzed by fear to move.

"And finally," Ms. Drake continued, "our last candidate is Lucy Beaner. Her vice presidential pick is Sam . . ." Ms. Drake's sigh echoed across Autumn Grove Intermediate School. "Lucy Beaner, report to the office immediately. You, too, Sam Righter."

Murmurs and whispers and not-so-whispery whispers bounced around the room as my legs, so eager to run and/or kick a moment before, suddenly didn't want to move at all and weighed about the same as elephant legs. I grabbed my backpack and trudged out the door.

Sam stood right outside the office door, waiting for

me, his face bright red and eyes shining, but not happy shiny. Hurt shiny. "Lucy." He rushed toward me. "Did you sign me up to be vice president and *not tell me?*"

I shrugged. "It doesn't matter. I withdraw."

"It does matter!" Sam yelled. (As much as Sam yells, which isn't really yelling at all. But it really felt like a yell.)

"It's not like you told me *you* were running!" I outright yelled.

"Because I didn't see you in time," Sam said. "It all happened when I went to Sheldon's house after school to talk about the Shelled Ones thing. We emailed Mr. Grayson, and he gave us an extension to submit our application."

"You should've told me."

"I should've told you that *I* decided to run?" Sam stepped back, shaking his head. "Don't you think *you* should've told me *you* decided I should run?"

I crossed my arms, all of a sudden more angry than ashamed. And then my mouth opened like a spigot and all that anger rushed out. "Sheldon only wants you to be president because you're suddenly popular!"

Sam's breath puffed out of his mouth. "Of course that's why. And he told me that's why. He doesn't think he could win without me, *and* he thinks I'll do a good job. He was honest. You should try it some time."

"Don't be mean!" I snapped. "I think you'll do a good job, too. And I tried to tell you—but you flaked on going to the wolf sanctuary and then you weren't here this morning—"

"Yeah, you were going to tell me that you already signed me up. As *vice* president," Sam snapped back.

"Because we're a pack—you and me! I'm Sascha and you're Ralph!"

"Why do you get to be Sascha all the time?" Sam asked. His eyes were angry slits.

"Because that's how we are! I'm more Sascha-ey," I said. "Sam, candidates have to do debates in front of the whole class. Think about it! You told me you hate to talk in front of people. We had to practice our wolf speech a thousand times before you could do it without a stomachache, and that was just our class!"

"So now you're telling me you don't think I can do it? Some friend."

"No, Sam, I think you'd be great. I just thought—"

"You know what? I don't want to hear it." He turned his back to me and opened the office door. "And you were trying to use me, too, only you're too scared to admit it."

I stepped forward, thinking he'd hold the door open for me. Instead, he just let it close behind him.

❖ ❖ ❖

Sam quickly told Ms. Drake what happened, that I had signed him up to be my vice president without checking with him. I just sat there, not speaking and, somehow, not crying or defending myself or anything. Ms. Drake dismissed Sam but told me to stay in her office. She sat back down at her desk, her neck stretching forward in that eagle way of hers and watching me. After a long, long silence, she asked that horrible parenty-principally question everyone hates: "Do you have anything to say for yourself?"

I shook my head.

Another long silence. "I suggest you try," Ms. Drake said.

"I don't want to run for president anymore." I stared out the window. Buses were beginning to line up. Another long pause.

"No," Ms. Drake said. She turned toward her computer and pointed to the door. "You may leave."

"What do you mean *no*?" I asked.

"No. I do not accept your withdrawal. I'd like you to go home, think about this, about what propelled you to throw your name into the mix to begin with, and read about the positions. In fact, I'd like you to spend the rest of the week doing this. At the end of this week, if you'd still like to withdraw, I'll accept your decision."

"I don't even have a running mate!"

"Technically, you don't need one. I'm sure someone would step up to be vice president if you can't choose a different friend."

"I don't have any other friends!"

"Now you're just exaggerating." Ms. Drake's fingers flew across the keyboard as she continued ignoring my emotional pain.

"I'm not going to change my mind." I stood.

"Lucy," Ms. Drake said, "I know you better than you think I do. And I know you're not a quitter."

Chapter Eleven

I trudged back to my locker, not even caring if I missed
the bus home.

Miss Parker might be a real superhero with super-
hearing based on how she somehow tuned into me being
in the hall. Her pretty, bright face popped out of the classroom doorway. "Get everything cleared up, Lucy?"

I shrugged and threw open my locker door. "Guess so."

"Great! Remember me telling you that I offered to
be student council adviser this year?" She bounced a
little. Miss Parker was seriously chipper for a teacher.
"Swing back into the classroom once you've gathered
your belongings and join Tom and me so I can give you
the manuals."

"I'd rather go into the evil clown pupil."

"Excuse me?" Miss Parker asked.

"Nothing. I'll be right there."

A few seconds later, I slouched into the seat next to Tom, who was smirking at me. "No running mate, huh?" he said. "Guess Righter forgot to tell you *he* was running for president."

I shifted so my shoulder was to Tom before the gravy-pea section of my thought maker blurted, *no, it was actually me who forgot to tell Sam.* Miss Parker handed me one of the manuals, already flipped open to the section about class president responsibilities. Presidents had to lead class meetings, attend school board meetings, be part of some PTO meetings, make sure the rest of the officers did their jobs. Miss Parker quickly went through those and added, "If one of you becomes president, you will represent our school wherever you go. It's part of the responsibility. Good luck to you both!"

I sighed and left the classroom, even though Tom stayed seated. He walked home, so he could stick around however long he wanted without worrying about missing the bus. In the hallway, I popped open my locker to throw in the manual. I wouldn't need to review it. I wasn't going to run.

Tom's booming voice trickled out to the hall. "Thanks

for saying good luck, but you should probably save that for Lucy."

Miss Parker's voice got hard. "I dislike that kind of talk."

"I'm just saying," Tom continued. "I mean, I've got a lot more friends than her, and I'm, like, the Bearcats hero. I mean, Sam, he's a competitor. He's a hero, too."

"I wouldn't underestimate Lucy. She's got impressive research and debate skills. I think she'd do a great job." *Miss Parker, I take back every mean thought I've ever had about you.*

"Yeah, but no one's going to vote for her. She's not a hero like me and Sam."

I snagged the manual back from the scraps of paper and empty snack wrappers cluttering the bottom of my locker and shoved it into my backpack.

❖ ❖ ❖

After school, Dad asked if I wanted to go for a walk. We used to go for long walks together every afternoon, but after Molly was born, that sort of faded away. I guess it was sort of like when Mom would snuggle under the covers with me and read a book. She used to do that every night, too; she said it was her favorite part of the day. It was the only thing that made bedtime bearable, except she always stopped reading just when something super exciting happened to one of the characters and I'd have to be at war with myself for the whole next day—wanting to know what happened but sticking by my morals, which dictate avoiding bedtime. At some point, she stopped reading to me. I don't even think we finished the last story. The poor character is still lost in the woods with just a hatchet. I don't know when it happened. I can't even really blame Molly. Maybe one night Mom was too tired or Molly too fussy. And then a day later, I got too mouthy and Mom sent me to bed without reading. Two days stretched into three, into four, into forever.

The same thing happened with Dad's walks. They just kind of faded away. I missed them when I thought about it, but when I walked in and saw Dad standing there, a big smile on his face and asking if I wanted to go for a walk, for some reason I said no.

I don't even know why.

Maybe it's because Molly was all bundled up, too, ready to slip into the stroller and go with us.

"I told April I'd go over to her house after school," I said.

"You could call her, though. Or go to her house after?" Dad asked, his smile wobbling a little at the corner.

"That's okay, Daddy-o," I said way too happy. "You and Molly go." I gave Molly a kiss on her little fluff head and then I had no choice but to drop my backpack and go to April's house.

Despite our plans to see each other every day after school, I barely had seen April since school had started (her ninja-style takedown of the bicycle thief aside). The park just wasn't as fun to go to since Sam's accident, and then homework started, and . . . I guess it was sort of like reading a book at night with Mom.

Mrs. Chester was on the front porch watering potted plants when I arrived. Most of them were crinkly and dry. I doubted the water was going to do much good at this point but kept that to myself. "Hey, Lucy," she said. "April's getting ready for karate practice."

"Oh," I said, not knowing if that meant I should go home or go inside. So I just stood there a second.

"Did you hear?" Mrs. Chester continued. "That thief April caught, he was part of a huge bike-stealing ring stretching all the way up into Boston!"

"She's a real hero," I mumbled.

"Sure is," Mrs. Chester said.

"'Sept for the bad part," cut in Scrappy, standing just behind the screen door. "Tell April's friend about the bad part."

Mrs. Chester sighed. "It's just temporary, Scrappy."

Scrappy threw open the screen door, I think just so I could see his crossed arms and angry face. "My bicycle is now evident."

"Evident?" I repeated.

He nodded, his big brown eyes going wide. "Evident. So I don't get it back."

"Evidence," Mrs. Chester corrected. "And you will get it back, after the trial."

"Which could take years and years," Scrappy yelped. "Guess I'll just have to walk *everywhere* for the rest of my whole life."

"Scrappy, you're being a bit dramatic." Mrs. Chester rolled her eyes in my direction as she tucked the watering can under a wicker table. "It might only be a few months."

Scrappy uncrossed his arms, slapped them against his side, and crossed them again. Behind him, I spotted April trotting down the stairs in her karate uniform. "Lucy!" she said and smiled so wide I could see her back teeth.

Suddenly I was so glad I had stopped by. "Hey, April!" I called back. "Do you have a minute?"

"Only a minute," Mrs. Chester piped in. "We have to leave in three minutes." She turned toward me, her mouth twitching with a smile. "Did April tell you? She's the sparring captain now. She has to be there early to warm up with Master Betsy so she can lead the class through drills."

"No," I mumbled. "She didn't tell me." I had stopped going to karate a few weeks earlier when Grandma finally admitted I wasn't sensei material. (I had kicked myself in my own head, which is actually kind of impressive, if you think about it.) For a mean moment, I was glad I quit when I did, so I never had to have April be one of my teachers.

"It's not a big deal," April said, her cheeks flushing.

"It *is* a big deal," Mrs. Chester corrected.

"Congratulations." I turned to head down the porch stairs. "I'll stop by another time."

"No!" April scurried after me. She squeezed my shoulder to make me turn around. "I have two minutes and thirty seconds! We'll have to talk quickly!"

"I can do that!" My mouth stretched into a smile almost as big as April's. I loved when she slipped and fell back into her quick-as-firecracker-and-just-as-loud way of speaking.

"Okay! Sam called after school. You're running for president?"

Smile gone. "Yeah. But I'm going to quit."

"Why would you do that? You'd be a great president!"

I squinted into April's face, trying to figure out if she was making fun of me. Her green eyes blinked solemnly back at me. "Do you think so?"

"I do!" April nodded as she spoke.

"Why?" I asked, sort of hating myself for digging for a compliment but also really wanting to know.

"Well, you notice when other people are feeling left out and figure out how to make them part of things. That's really important. And you're not afraid to stand up for yourself or what you believe."

"That's true," I whispered.

"And when you make mistakes, you fix them." I glanced at April. Her eyebrow popped up and her eyes bore into mine.

"I need to fix this with Sam, don't I?"

April's eyebrow was going to shoot straight off her head like a rubber band soon. "I'm telling you, you're class president material," she said. "Once you fix this."

"April's class president! She would know!" Scrappy burst in from the doorway.

"You're class president?" I asked. "You never told me."

April shrugged. "It's not a big deal."

"Yes, it is!" I stomped my foot. "Why wouldn't you tell me that? First you don't say anything about being team captain at Miss Betsy's. Then I find out you broke up a whole bike-stealing ring from your mom. Now you didn't even tell me about being class president at your fancy new school. You've been there for a week, and you're already class president!"

April's face settled into something scary smooth. Her bright, happy smile vanished. "First of all, my school isn't *fancy*. It's just different. There are ten other kids in my class. On the first day, the teacher asked if anyone wanted to be president and I raised my hand. Not a big deal. And secondly, I didn't tell you about those things because I didn't want to sound like I was bragging or something. You get weird, Lucy, about stuff like that."

"What do you mean, *weird*?" But for some reason, when I said it, the word made my whole body shimmy, which was, well, weird.

She tilted her head in my direction.

"Oh, come on!" I stomped again.

April sighed. "You're always comparing yourself to everyone else in the pack. It's easier not to tell you stuff. That's *not* presidential, but I think you could work on it."

"Of course I'm comparing myself! Everyone else is a hero!"

April rolled her eyes. She crossed her arms, for a second looking a lot like Scrappy. "Stop it."

"I'm serious! You go solving crimes again. Sam throws toddlers to safety. Even Shemanda are off saving turtles. And then there's me!"

Now April's face was flushing red. "Stop it!"

"Stop what?" I snapped back.

"Stop whining! You want to be president? Then be president! Stop crying about how much harder it is for you than everyone else, as if it was *lucky* that I had to go to a different school just to be seen, or that Scrappy's bike got stolen or those kids almost got run over or Sam crushed his arm. Stop it!" April was so angry that her lips turned white while she yelled and her hands curled into fists at her side. "You're a good friend most of the time, Lucy, but when you're not, you're *awful*."

I stepped backward, stumbling down the stairs.

But April wasn't finished. "You want to be a hero? Then be one!"

"April?" Mrs. Chester's voice was cautious. "It's time to go."

I turned and ran from April's house, ignoring her calling my name.

Now I did it.

Now I didn't have anyone.

You'd think I'd have gotten used to this feeling by now.

❖ ❖ ❖

I turned toward home, but just as I walked up the road toward my driveway, I spotted Dad. He must've decided against the stroller, instead putting Molly in the back-pack carrier, so her body faced outward. For a second, I thought about running ahead and joining them, but then I remembered that my face was red and streaky from crying. If I ran to Dad, I'd have to explain that April and I got into a fight, and I'd have to say it was because I was jealous, and I'd have to say that being jealous cost me my two best friends. And Mom and Dad were under the impression that I had already cleared with Sam the whole running for vice president thing, and I'd have Dad's disappointed face to deal with on top of everything else. So I ducked behind a bush and watched Molly's chubby legs kicking and arms waving. Dad paused by the tree in our neighbor's yard and plucked a leaf from it. "Brown," he told Molly. "Do you want to touch it?"

Gently he ran Molly's hand along the leaf. Her fist closed over it, crumbling the brittle leaf into pieces. Dad pulled open Molly's hand and blew the broken pieces into the air, making Molly giggle. Her fist opened and closed for more. "Let's go to that tree," Dad said and pointed down the street to a maple tree. "It's yellow. *Yellow*," he repeated slowly.

"Gaga," Molly replied.

I waited for Dad and Molly to disappear down the bend before taking off in the opposite direction.

Thanks to Dad's walks, I pretty much knew all of the roads in town. A route we used to go on a lot stretched north of town, past the park, by the water tower and beside a long, long cornfield. It was a quiet and bright walk, and it gave me time to think. I didn't like the thoughts I had, though. Thoughts first about how everyone was leaving me—April, Grandma, Sam, and, in some ways, even Mom and Dad. Those thoughts stretched thin as the strips of clouds above me until they morphed into something altogether new. Something that whispered I was whining. It sounded a lot like April.

The road ended at the end of the cornfield. Now I could turn around and head home the same way or turn left and loop around. Turning left and looping instead of turning around was the prettier walk, but it went through a wooded section that, when Dad was with me, I usually thought was beautiful but which looked full of shadows now. I checked my phone. The battery was fully charged. *Heroes are brave*, I reminded myself.

I bit my lip again and turned left.

Chapter Twelve

The woods sucked up all the sunlight, sending shadows across the road. I realized a few things. First, no one knew where I was. Dad thought I was with April; April thought I had gone home. If I went missing, swallowed up by an evil clown pupil, no one would think to look for me on this road on the other side of town. Second, while open cornfields might make you realize your mistakes, shadowy woods liked to really rub those mistakes in. I felt so small walking under the big pine and maple trees on either side of the road.

We've got to fix this, I told myself as firmly as possible. April was right; I had been whining. But she was wrong that I had been jealous over the terrible things that happened to my friends. When Sheldon finally makes his time machine to study the dinosaurs, I'd totally make a pit stop back a few weeks ago at the park and keep Sam and the toddlers from being in that car's way. I hated that my friend was hurting, and not just physically but inside, too, about gymnastics. And I wasn't jealous that Scrappy's bike was stolen.

But that didn't mean I wasn't jealous at all. I was. *You're jealous too much of the time,* my thought maker spat out. It was never a good sign when it started talking to me in the singular like that instead of the we're-in-this-together way it usually operated.

I was jealous, I realized, not about the things that happened to my friends, but what they had done. They had looked for ways to help without even pausing to think about it. They just did it. They just helped.

I had to apologize to Sam and to April. Maybe they wouldn't listen. *We probably wouldn't,* my thought maker butt in. I mentally fist-bumped it for going back to plural. But even if Sam and April didn't accept it, I had to apologize and do better. I had to be like them—I had to look for ways to help and just do it.

I could be a hero, too.

And maybe, just maybe, I could be president.

I *wanted* to be president. I really, really wanted it.

Maybe the good friend thing to do would be to quit so Sam could be president. Maybe I didn't stand a chance against Tom. But the thing is, I always knew I'd recognize my awesome when I found it. And I *knew, knew, knew* that I could be an awesome president. I'd find ways to help other people, not just turtles like Sheldon planned to do (but I'd help turtles, too). I'd put myself out there and stand up for what was right, and I didn't mind being in the spotlight like Sam did. And I'd be nice to people, unlike jerkface Tom.

So what if no one liked me right now? When Eleanor Roosevelt became First Lady, no one really liked her, either. But she became a leader anyway, and soon enough, people got behind her.

I could be president.

I wasn't going to quit.

Wouldn't you know it, some sunlight fought its way through the trees, poking like golden spears through the shadows. Next thing I knew, I was skipping down the road, happy to be alone (but even happier no one could see me skipping). It felt good to have made a decision.

Then the road dipped downhill and my skipping felt like flying. It was amazing! It was incredible!

It was out of control!

How could skipping go so wrong so quickly? The hill was a lot steeper than I remembered. Somehow, I had forgotten that every time we walked it, Dad had said it was a good thing we were going downhill instead of up, how he always said something about how scary it'd be to drive down in the winter. *Try skipping it, Dad!* That's what I'd say next time. If I still had a mouth attached to my face, that is. I was like a human skipping snowball catapulting down this hill of death! I threw out my arms to get some wind resistance and tried to stiffen my legs, but they didn't even land on the pavement before shooting up in different directions. My hair flopped into my face and into my open screaming mouth as I careened down the hill. My feet skidded along the loose gravel by the side of the road and I knew this was it. I was going to face-plant. I was going to land at the bottom, look back up the hill, and see my mouth somewhere in the middle.

I squeezed my eyes shut as no part of me touched the ground. For just a second, I was an astronaut, floating in midair. And then, *boom!* Gravity.

Then, I lay sprawled at the bottom of the hill like a starfish, wondering if I still had a face but not sure if it was a good idea to lift my hand and find out.

Who knows how long I would've sprawled there

on the gravel, but then I heard something completely terrifying.

Something was eating my face. "Nom, nom, nom. Nomnomnom," it chewed.

My eyes shot open. *Good! We still have eyes!* My hands flew to my face. *Phew!* Still had a face. But *something* was definitely being eaten. I pushed myself up to look around. Standing next to me was a big gray goat with two spiky little horns, bulging blue eyes, and an enormous bumpy gut. "Nom, nom, nomnom."

"What are you eating, goat?" I scrambled to my feet, my hands patting my hips and legs to make sure all my parts were present. I winced as my elbows flexed. I brushed some of the gravel out from where it was embedded into the skin there. My bum was bruised, I could tell, but nothing seemed broken. Dad probably was home from his walk with Molly; I'd text him to come and get me. I reached in my back pocket for my phone. Nothing. I squinted up the giant hill for a flash of my phone's blue case. Nothing.

"Have you seen my phone, goat?" And that's when I saw the blue case. IT WAS IN THE GOAT'S MOUTH!

"Nom, nom, nom."

"Are you eating *my phone*, goat?"

"Nom."

"Give me back my phone!" But the goat didn't even blink. Just worked its jaw in little circles around my phone. Mom was going to kill me! She had gotten me a super industrial case that you could drive over and it'd keep the phone safe. "It's Lucy-proof," she had said. But was it goat-proof?

"Nom, nom, nom."

I wrapped my fingers around the edge of the phone hanging out of the goat's mouth and yanked. Thanks to goopy goat slobber, my fingers slipped right off the phone, and there I was on my bruised bum all over again. "You shouldn't eat a phone, goat!"

The goat's lips fluttered and it made a noise that sounded a lot like when I squeeze air from a sagging balloon. And it kept right on chewing my phone. "Goat," I growled. Goat made the sagging balloon noise again.

I wiped my fingers on my pant legs and grabbed the phone again. Yank! "Phones," yank, "are *not,*" yank, "for eating," yank, "goat!" My feet were planted in the grass beside the road and I was pulling on the phone so hard, I felt like two sides of a triangle. And just when I made that realization, Goat let loose. Bam! My poor bum would never be the same.

"Bllleeeerrrrpppp," said Goat.

"Oh, shut it," I said. "Eat some grass or something."

Goat wandered toward me, sniffing at my shoelaces.

"Where's your human?" I got to my feet and looked around. I couldn't see any houses around, thanks to all the trees, but there was an old, rusted metal fence lining a clearing across the road. The grass was worn away in patches and a little shed-like building was in the middle.

"Is that your home, goat?"

"Nay," said Goat. It stomped forward, its big lips stretching out and around a lock of my hair.

"Don't even think about it," I said. "Go home."

"Blleeerp."

I walked over to the fence, Goat trotting beside me. The fence looked super old and rusty. I doubted Goat could live there. Half of it was falling down. I wiped more goat slobber into my pant leg to clean off my phone and call home. Only problem? No reception. Not even one little bar. "Lollipop farts, Goat. What are we going to do?"

"Nom, nom, nom."

"Stop eating my hair! It's attached to my head." I yanked my hair out of Goat's mouth. "Well, listen. I'll just go on home and tell my dad you're out here. We'll come back for you. Okay?"

"Bllleeerrp?" Goat nudged my ribs with his face. I tried to push his head back, but when I did, he twisted so I was scratching behind his ear. "Burrrlglum," he said in a super soft goat voice.

"Does that feel good?" I scratched behind his other ear. Again he made the happy goat sound. His hair was coarse, sort of like petting thin straw, but it was also weirdly oily so my fingers now were slobbered and greasy. But Goat made the happy sound again and I knew I couldn't leave him. Besides, what do heroes do? They take action! "Let's go, Goat," I said and led the way back to my house.

By the time we got back to town, about two inches of hair was missing on the left side of my head and Goat kept nudging my hand to scratch between his ears. That was okay, though. When I scratched, he closed his eyes and I didn't have to see his flat pupils. They made my knees hurt. "No offense, Goat," I said, "but your eyes are creepy."

The further we walked, the more I realized what I was doing. I had seen a starving goat destined for a life of desolation in the woods and flung myself down a hill toward it. (Fine, so those events are in reverse order, strictly speaking, but both were true.) And then, instead of leaving him there all alone, I befriended the goat and rescued him. I bet he could live in our backyard. Dad wouldn't have to mow anymore! And Goat would probably become the focus of a major newspaper article.

I could see the headline now. *Local girl saves starving lonely goat, feeds it her own hair.* I bet reporters would fight for interviews with the brave girl who saved the lonely goat.

One of my neighbors, a little old lady who was always sitting on her front porch, stood as I walked by with Goat. "Good afternoon, Mrs. Chambers," I said. "Lovely day, huh?"

"Is that a goat?" she asked.

"Why, yes," I replied, patting Goat on the neck. "I'm saving him."

"Oh." Mrs. Chambers leaned off her porch railing. "That looks like Tomkin, Farmer Lemmings's goat."

"No." I shook my head. "He was lost and starving and so he ate my hair and now I'm taking him home."

"Hmm." Mrs. Chambers went into her house. As Goat and I walked past, I saw the curtain flicker in her window.

Goat spent way too long gnawing on the dandelions by the creek behind my house, so I took off one of my shoelaces and made a little lasso around his neck to prod him along. We circled around to the front of my house. "Dad!" I called. "Come quick! I saved a goat!"

At the same moment Dad threw open the screen door to step out with Molly still strapped to his chest, a siren so loud and close it made both me and Goat jump a couple inches in the air—which really hurt considering Goat was nibbling more of my hair at the time—erupted just behind me. I whipped around to see a police car pulling into the driveway. The window lowered and an officer popped out a megaphone. "Step away from the goat!"

"Excuse me?" I yelled.

"Step away from the goat!"

I dropped the shoelace lasso and took a giant step away from Goat. Goat yanked back on the clump of hair still in his mouth. "I can't!" I yelped.

The officer got out of the car, though the lights were still flashing.

"What's going on here?" Dad asked, rushing toward me.

The police officer, a tall, wide man with just a few sprigs of hair across his shiny head but a very full mustache, whipped out a notebook from his back pocket. "We've had reports of a stolen goat."

"But I didn't steal this goat. He followed me!"

The officer's eyes flicked from the shoelace around Goat's neck back to me.

"It's not what it looks like!"

"It looks like you stole a goat," Dad whispered.

"He followed me! I'm saving him!"

"Bllleeeerrrgh!" screeched Goat as another car pulled into the driveway. It was an old white pickup truck. When the old man behind the wheel got out of the car, Goat—with a chunk of my hair still in his traitor mouth—lurched forward, screeching so loud Molly started to cry.

"Tomkin!" the old man bellowed.

"Bleeeergh!" Goat bellowed back as they ran toward each other, Goat dragging me along with a mouthful of hair. The old man hugged the goat around the neck.

The passenger side of the truck opened and closed as someone else got out but I concentrated on pulling strands of goat-slobbered hair free from Goat's—I mean, Tomkin's—mouth.

"Did you steal my grandpa's goat?" Snort, snort.

Yep. Standing in front of me was Tom.

The officer cleared his throat. "Do you want to press goat-napping charges, Mr. Lemmings?"

The old man raised his head from Tomkin the Goat's neck. "Charges?"

"I didn't steal the goat!" I screeched. "He ate my phone. And then he ate my hair. I *saved* him!"

Mr. Lemming scratched between Tomkin's ears, making the goat erupt in happy groans. But it was like the ear scratching made Tomkin suddenly remember me. He whipped around and buried his head under my hand so I'd scratch, too. Farmer Lemmings looked from the goat back to me. "Nah, I don't think she meant to steal my Tomkin."

"I didn't steal him!" I shouted again.

Dad stepped forward. "I'm not sure what's going on here, but I'm sure my daughter would never intentionally goat-nap."

"I just can't believe she'd rip down Tomkin's fence like that," Farmer Lemmings said.

Farmer Lemmings and the police officer both looked at me top to bottom. Dad did, too, with a big sigh. So, okay, my pants were ripped at the knees and coated in goat slobber. My arms had scrapes all up and down them that hadn't hurt at all until just then, when they turned to fire. My hair was lopsided and chewed upon. I was pretty sure there was a nice thick layer of dirt around my face. I looked like someone who tore down a fence to steal a goat.

"He broke through his fence." I focused on Dad, not wanting jerkface Tom Lemmings to see the tears in my eyes. I had to get all my words out before my stupid tears messed them up, so I opened my mouth and everything poured right out like a word volcano spewing all over me. "I swear it, Dad. I fell down the hill because I was skipping because I want to be president and then this goat was eating my face, but it was really my phone, and then he wanted to eat my hair and I said, 'Stop, goat,' but he said, 'Blleeergh,' and then he followed me because I'm a hero and I saved him and none of this is happening the way it's supposed to! Where are the newspaper reporters?"

Dad, the officer, and Farmer Lemmings all blinked at me. Next to them, Tom snort-laughed, but I wouldn't look at him. That is, until I heard something that sounded a lot like the click of a camera. Then I lunged, swatting Tom's phone into the dirt. "Stop it!" I screamed. Only Tom didn't have a Tomkin-proof phone.

❖ ❖ ❖

A few minutes later, the pickup truck slowly backed out of the driveway. Farmer Lemmings drove with the window down, his hand outstretched and holding a length of rope tied around Tomkin's neck. He drove about a half mile per hour down the road and back to the farm. Tom glared out the window at me, his nostrils flared and eyes narrowed.

The police officer scribbled things in a little notebook. "Look, kid. You're a minor so none of this is going to be on your record, and Farmer Lemmings opted not to charge you for goat-napping or destruction of his grandson's phone. You're lucky."

"Yes, sir," I mumbled.

Dad put his hand on my shoulder with a big sigh. Turning me toward him, he added, "And Lucy will be paying for Tom's new phone with her allowance and chore money."

The next day, I saw that I finally did make it into the newspaper. Mom pointed it out, a small paragraph in the daily police log. "Officer responded to what appeared to be a goat-napping underway. Minor-aged culprit promises to avoid future encounters with farm animals."

Mom laughed, spreading out the newspaper around where I perched on the kitchen table to catch the clipped hair she trimmed from my right side to match my goat-gnawed left. "I'd say all's well that ends well, Lucy. You needed a haircut anyway."

Dad walked by holding Molly. "Think they'll give you a hard time at school about this?"

"Yes," I whimpered. "Can't I be homeschooled now? *Please.*"

"Nay," Mom said, stretching out the word to sound like Tomkin.

Dad piped in, "I'm sure it won't 'goat' out of hand."

My life is ruined.

Chapter Thirteen

Sam was by my locker when I got to school. "Sam!" I smiled for the first time since the goat-napping accident. "I thought you hated me."

"I don't *hate* you, Lucy. I'm just mad at you."

"But we're still friends?" I asked, trying hard to keep my voice from shaking.

Sam looked at his shoes. "Did you really steal a goat?" he whispered.

"It was an accident."

"How do you accidentally steal a goat?"

"Wait!" I slammed shut my locker door. "How did you find out?"

Sam's eyes slid to the other side of the hall. There hung an enormous poster with the words *Don't vote for a goat-napper!* And—lollipop farts!—my picture. Not just any picture, either. It was me with my Tomkin-styled hair, covered in dirt, next to a police officer, and lunging forward. Guess Tomkin wasn't able to destroy the camera part of Tom's phone. I screamed. It sounded a lot like Tomkin.

Sam sighed and walked over, swiping the poster from the wall and crumpling it up. "I took down four other ones, but I think Tom counted on that. He keeps putting up more."

My hand flopped toward Sam, like it wanted to grab his hand or something. I made it fall back against my side. *Fix it*, I told myself. "I'm sorry, Sam. Not about the goat—that was an accident. I mean about what I did to you. I really screwed up. I should've talked to you."

Sam nodded, but still didn't look at me. Instead, he focused on the crumpled-up goat-napper poster. "I'm still angry."

"I know," I said. "And it might make you more angry, but I'm not going to drop out. I'm going to run for president, too."

Now Sam's face did shoot up to mine. "Don't you think I could do a good job?"

"I think you'd do a great job. But I want to do it, too."

Sam took a step backward. "You're going to run against me and Sheldon?"

"I think I found my awesome, Sam. I think I could do a good job."

"I can't believe you're doing this."

I breathed in through my nose. "I should've talked to you beforehand, okay? I know. But you and Sheldon didn't tell me you were running, either."

Sam opened his mouth to speak and then mashed it shut again. "Okay," he said at last. "I'll quit."

"No way!" I said. "No way. You can't quit. If you quit, then I'll quit."

"That doesn't make any sense," Sam said. "If we both run, then one of us loses."

"Yes, but if we both run, one of us might win."

Sam did the open-and-then-shut-mouth thing again. "That kind of makes sense."

I smiled.

"Okay," Sam said. "Let the best man win."

"Or woman."

"Goat-napper!" someone shouted as walked by.

Sam and I both howled—like the pack we were—at the same time. At least, that's what I had hoped would happened. What really happened is that I howled. Alone.

"Sam!" I snapped.

He yelped a little.

"You're still mad, aren't you?"

Sam shrugged. "I'll get over it."

"I'm sorry," I said again.

"I know." Sam sighed as the bell rang again. "Even if this hadn't happened, I think I need some time kind of by myself."

"What do you mean?" For a second, it felt like I was falling down that hill all over again, even as I stood right there in the hallway.

"I'm just . . . I don't know. I don't even know." His casted arm jerked out a little.

"It's just an arm that's broken," I said, wincing when I realized my voice sounded shaky again, like it knew the words it was putting forth weren't true before I did. I cleared my throat. "It's just an arm. It's not all of you."

But Sam? He did look broken just then.

"I'll see you later, Lucy," he said and walked away, right past another goat-napping poster.

❖ ❖ ❖

In front of the old section of the playground, Shemanda

sat at a long table. Yellow tape circled the swing set and old monkey bars, keeping everyone else back. A big poster hung from the front of the table. *Vote for a hero! Be a hero! Save the Shelled Ones with Sam and Sheldon.* In the middle was a drawing of a big turtle. I recognized the glittery crayon styling. April. So the rest of the pack was getting together without me, probably while I was being hurled to my almost death down the hill.

Stop feeling sorry for yourself, my thought maker snapped. "Nice poster," I said to Sheldon.

"Thanks!" he said. He and Amanda exchanged a glance and I knew they had been talking about me.

"Just so you know," I said, "if I become president, I'll save the turtles, too."

Sheldon's face split into a big grin. "Thanks, Lucy. I knew you would."

Amanda pointed to a chair beside her. "Want to sit with us?"

"Are you sure?" There were only three chairs.

"Yeah, Sam said he's spending recess in the library."

"Oh," I said, not sure what stung about that comment more—that Sheldon knew where Sam was and I didn't or that Sam would rather spend recess with Mrs. Fredericks than his pack. I settled into the seat at the same moment that Sheldon popped to his feet.

"Hey!" he yelled and waved his arms. A soccer ball had rolled under the yellow tape into the turtle excavation zone and the kid who had kicked it was trotting toward it. "Stop!" Sheldon zoomed over toward the ball. "I'll handle this." Gingerly, Sheldon tiptoed over the mulch to the ball. The soundtrack to *Mission Impossible* played in my head.

Amanda, who had been coloring in a turtle on another poster, half stood to keep an eye on Sheldon. Really she had been keeping an eye on the other people, making sure they left Sheldon alone. The green crayon she had been using rolled off the table and into the grass. When I bent down to get it, I noticed something odd.

"Amanda," I blurted, "your legs!"

"What?" She sat back down and stretched her legs out in front of her. "Yeah, I nicked a few spots."

"A few?" Amanda's legs each had a half-dozen band-aids, most of them around the knees.

She shrugged. "Knees are tricky to shave. My dad says I should use his electric razor but then it just looks like I gave my legs a buzz cut."

"Shave? You shave your legs?"

"You don't?" Amanda tilted her head at me. Amanda glanced at my legs. Quickly I tucked my skirt over my knees. Suddenly the brownish-blonde hair I had never really noticed before felt thick as fleece tights.

"It's not a big deal," Amanda said.

"It kind of is," I whispered back. "I haven't even talked to my mom about it. Did you bring it up to yours or did she mention it to you?"

Amanda rolled her eyes. "I didn't check with anyone. I just did it."

"You can do that?" I asked.

She shrugged again.

"I'm pretty sure my mom would freak out. Or want to talk about it. All she wants to do is talk about stuff lately." I picked up the crayon and started coloring in the turtle. "She's all 'soon you'll be embracing your womanhood' and 'wear deodorant, trust me.' She even snuck a . . . device . . . into my backpack."

Amanda was pressing her mouth together so tight her lips were white. It was her angry face, but by now I knew not to take it personally. Probably someone was getting too close to the excavation zone and she wasn't even listening to me. Another crayon rolled off the table. When I picked it up, I accidentally-on-purpose brushed against Amanda's leg. It was as soft as a flower petal, unlike my chimpanzee skin.

"Did you just touch my leg?" she snapped.

"No." I turned back to the poster. "I'll check the basket for leg shaving razors."

"The basket?"

Mom had recently made a big deal out of announcing that there was a basket under the bathroom sink filled with "supplies" if I ever needed anything new. I think you know what I mean there. "She filled it with a bunch of stuff for when I have," I glanced around and then hissed the horrible p word. The one that rhymes with ew-burty.

"She did?" Amanda's hands fisted. "What's in the basket?"

"You know," I said to Amanda rather than answer, "it's not all that shocking these turtles are endangered."

"Because their habitat is taken over by humans?" Amanda kept her eyes on Sheldon. I knew if anyone gave him a hard time, she'd plow over to him immediately.

"I was thinking more because the mama turtle wasn't made for momming. I mean, she pops out the eggs in a playground then leaves? What kind of mom does that?"

"One who doesn't even want to be a mom."

I shuddered. "Thank goodness we're not turtles."

Next to me, Amanda shuddered, too. But she didn't stop. Her shoulders wobbled up and down, up and down. And then her face sort of folded in on itself and a hissing noise slipped through her nose, and then something so shocking happened I had to rub the heels of my hands into my eyeballs to make sure they weren't tricking me.

Amanda cried.

That's not even right, since it was so much more than that. She wasn't just crying. She was all-out sobbing. Amanda bent her head on the table and cried and cried. "Um, Amanda?" I whispered. "Are you okay?"

"My mom's a turtle," she whimpered.

"What?" I tried to remember if I had ever met Amanda's mom. I had never been over to her house. Whenever we saw each other outside of school, we met at the park or at someone else's house. I don't know why, but it hadn't ever even entered my mind to go to Amanda's house or meet her parents. I thought hard, trying to remember school parties or concerts when parents came in. But I couldn't remember ever having seen them.

Amanda raised her head a little. She looked so different when she was sad. Angry Amanda, I was used to seeing. That was pretty much her usual face—round with a straight-line mouth; a small, straight nose; and narrow, brown eyes under thick, straight eyebrows. This sad face was hard to see. Not because she was ugly or anything. (Amanda's really pretty when she smiles and her cheeks lift up and her eyes get twinkly. In fact, once she was smiling in the hall between classes and three people rammed into each other as she passed because they were so distracted by her happy face.) It was hard to see her sadness because she fell into it so fully. I don't know if that makes sense, but the sadness, while it was the first I had ever seen it, didn't look like it was new. Her eyebrows cinched together thanks to a deep crease between them. Her mouth dipped at the corners and so did her eyes. The worst, though, was seeing her bottom lip quivering. "My mom's a turtle," she said again.

"What do you mean?" I asked. And then I remembered. I gasped. "Did she leave you at a playground?"

Amanda shook her head, loosening more tears. "At the Days of Yonder Faire. She's a fortune-teller. My dad was a sword swallower."

"What?" I rubbed my ears this time. The Days of Yonder Faire came to town every fall. Mom always wanted Dad to dress up like a knight to match the peasant dresses she and I wore. Even though the Faire was months and months from now, I had spied Mom shopping online for one of those tall pointed princess hats for Molly.

Amanda wiped at her cheeks. "My mom left me when I was a baby. They were supposed to quit the Faire, but when it moved on to the next town, Mom went with it and left me and Dad."

"Amanda, I'm so sorry," I said. I patted her back a little. Most people, I guess, would've given her a hug, but Amanda's not really the hugging type. She wasn't the pat-on-the-back type, either, I guess, since she almost immediately popped to her feet.

"I've got to go." She leaned in close. "If you tell anyone my mom's a turtle, Lucy Beaner—"

I threw up my hands. "I wouldn't!"

Amanda stormed into the school, her face back to its familiar angry straightness.

"Where's Amanda going?" Sheldon squinted toward his girlfriend's retreating back.

"Um, bathroom," I said.

"She looked kind of—"

"Is that person heading toward the excavation zone?" I pointed randomly behind Sheldon, who whipped around and took off with arms flailing.

❖ ❖ ❖

"Her mom's a turtle, huh?" Grandma gently pushed the porch swing forward later that night. I sat next to her, my body curled into hers and legs up on the bench while she did all of the swinging. I tried not to pay attention to the way the porch light made the diamond on her finger flicker.

Grandma and I had been sitting on the porch for more than an hour. I had homework to do, but the only thing I could think about was what happened with Amanda that afternoon. It was getting pretty chilly out on the porch, but Grandma was soft and warm next to me. "And you never knew any of this about Amanda?"

Even though it was dark, I shook my head instead of answering.

"It must be pretty hard not to have a mom around," Grandma said. "Your mom, she never had her dad. And that was tough, on both of us. I imagine it's even harder for a girl your age to not have a mom around."

"What do you mean 'a girl my age'?"

Grandma nudged my side. "You know, going through pub—"

"Don't you say it! Don't you even say it!" I pressed my hands over my ears.

Grandma yelled it into the quiet night sky. "Puberty! You're going through puberty!"

"Grandma!"

"Well, it's true, toots. I'm sure you've noticed some . . . changes." Her furry eyebrow popped up.

I folded my arms over my chest. "No."

"Lucy."

I shook my head.

"Pretty soon you're going to get your per—"

"Lalalalalalala!" I crammed my fingers into my ears before she could say the word that should only ever be punctuation.

I felt Grandma's chest rise and fall as she let out a deep breath. When I felt it was safe, I lowered my hands. The truth is, I had been noticing changes, just not necessarily with me. I still looked and felt the same as always. But April? She suddenly looked more glamorous, more like a teenager than a girl. And Amanda? Her clothes weren't so baggy anymore and not because she had gained weight, either. It was like her weight had been redistributed, if you know what I mean. I don't really want to talk about it, but I think you know what I mean.

"Well," Grandma said, "if you ever want to talk about anything—"

"Ugh! Why do you and Mom keep asking me that?"

Grandma shifted in her seat, planting her feet to stand. "Would you rather no one ask?" She put a finger over my lips to keep me from speaking. "Think about it. Really think about it. Then think about Amanda."

Grandma sat back and swung a little more. I rested my head against her soft side. "Maybe Amanda would want to have a sleepover this weekend."

"That's a good idea, toots."

Chapter Fourteen

"Goat, I've got problems."

Tomkin laid his head over his fence, his lips stretching to nibble on a piece of my hair.

Visiting the goat probably was a bad idea, but I'd gone for walks after school almost every day and always ended up by his fence. Farmer Lemmings had pulled up in the pickup truck the first day I had showed up and just nodded when he saw me scratching Tomkin between the ears. "He's a good boy, isn't he?" Farmer Lemmings had said and pointed out a rusted green tackle box next to the fence. It was filled with candy canes. "Tomkin's favorite candy," Farmer Lemmings said.

"His *favorite* candy? Tomkin has had a lot of candy?"

Farmer Lemmings shrugged as he unwrapped a

candy cane. "Well, how else would we know which candy is his favorite?"

Farmer Lemmings handed me the peeled candy cane. A rumbling moan bubbled up from deep inside Tomkin. His creepy bulgy eyes rolled and his lips quivered and his whole body leaned in toward the treat.

"Wow, he eats them the way I eat spaghetti noodles!" Tomkin slurped the candy cane back so fast he caught my fingertips, too. I wiped them on my jeans. "How many can he have?"

Farmer Lemmings scratched the back of his head with another candy cane. "Oh, he's been having about four a day for the past twelve years."

"Tomkin is twelve years old?"

"Yep." Farmer Lemmings handed me the next peeled candy cane. "A little more than a year older than you and the other Tomkin, huh?"

"Wait. What?" And then I screamed "ouch" because apparently I didn't give up the candy cane fast enough for Tomkin, considering he chomped down on my finger.

"Watch the teeth, now," Farmer Lemmings said.

"No, I mean about the other Tomkin. Do you have another goat?"

"No, no." Farmer Lemmings chuckled. "I mean the

boy Tomkin. He's in your class, isn't he? Tells me he's going to be class president."

"Wait," I said again. "Tom is named after a goat?"

"'Course," he said and handed me another candy cane.

I hadn't told anyone that Tom was named after a goat and that his actual name was Tomkin. I didn't think Tomkin the Goat deserved to be associated with Tomkin the Human. And then there was, of course, the fact that my total friends list was down to two and one was my other opponent and the other his girlfriend. Sam still wasn't talking to me much and I hadn't seen April since she told me I was awful.

I snuck Tomkin an extra candy cane.

"Blllergh," he said as thanks.

"I've got to talk to April again, but I don't know how," I told Tomkin the Goat. I don't know why exactly, but I knew it'd be wrong to have a sleepover with Amanda and not invite April. It'd be like cheating on our friendship somehow. They were both my friends, but a sleepover with just Amanda would be like declaring that April wasn't as good a friend.

"Nnnnaaargl," Tomkin the Goat said.

"I know, I know. I'm making it all so complicated."

He nudged me with his horn.

"Yes, of course. I have plenty of other things to worry about. Like the fact that Grandma is getting married and moving away in a stupid RV. And that Amanda's probably going to want to talk about devices and supplies and all that stuff that everyone wants to talk about but me."

"Bbaaabergl."

"You're right, Tomkin the Goat. You're right. I can't forget about the presidential race."

Every day I saw more goat-napping posters hanging in the halls. Every day someone else would come up to me and ask if it was true, if I really had stolen Tom's grandfather's goat. The latest was at lunch today. A kid named Kyle, a fellow solo eater in the cafeteria, asked me if I really had tried to steal Tomkin. Amanda, the only other one sitting with me since Sheldon and Sam were making posters in the library, had snorted and tried to give me a fist-bump. She always did that whenever anyone brought up the alleged goat-napping.

"No," I had whispered. "It was an accident."

"How do you accidentally steal a goat?" Kyle half laughed as he said it like this was all a big joke.

"Listen, okay," I said, "I saw the goat standing by itself at the side of the road. It followed me. It looked lonely. I couldn't just leave it there, being lonely, all by itself. It needed a friend, or something. So I brought it home. I didn't steal it."

"Oh," Kyle said. His ears turned pink.

Miss Parker's high heels smacked the floor as she moved closer to us. "Why did the goat's loneliness bother you?" she asked me, a little smile flickering around her mouth.

"No one wants to be lonely," I said. "It's the worst."

"Sounds like that's an issue that would be important to you as president," Miss Parker said.

"Goat loneliness?" Kyle asked. "Is that a big issue here?" Kyle had just moved to Autumn Grove from Missouri, so I could understand his confusion.

"No," Miss Parker said with a laugh. "Student loneliness. As in, students who might have trouble finding a friend to play with at recess or sit with at lunch."

Kyle's face flushed a little more and Amanda snorted again. "Yeah," Amanda said, "I think Lucy might have some experience there." Both of us laughed and howled a little.

"If you were president," Miss Parker continued, "what would you do for students who are lonely?"

I glanced around the room. Some tables were overflowing with students who had snagged chairs from other tables and crowded together. A few tables only had one or two people, like Kyle's and mine. "When I was having a rough time—I mean, the *last time* I was having a rough time—I formed a pack. A group of solo eaters, like me. We found things we really like to do together or stuff we care about, like wolves."

"And turtles!" Amanda cut in.

"Yeah, and turtles. So maybe, if I were president, I'd help other fifth graders find each other, too."

"How would you do that?" Kyle asked.

Kyle wore a Captain America T-shirt, which reminded me of Miss Parker's LARPing life. "Well, maybe we could have clubs? Like maybe a superhero or comic book club?" I glanced at Amanda. "And maybe a club for animal issues. They could meet after school or during lunch."

"How about one for animal *and* anger issues?" Amanda asked.

"I don't know how many—" I bit off the rest of the sentence as Amanda's face set in anger and she started chanting *kumbaya* under her breath. "Sure," I said instead. "Or maybe a yoga club?"

"Sweet," Amanda said. She held out her fist for another bump.

Kyle smiled. "Clubs. I like that idea."

"Maybe a women's issues club," said a girl at the

table behind us. She had a bright blue streak of hair and a *Down with the Patriarchy* T-shirt.

"A running club!" said the girl next to her.

"Sure," I said. "I think those are all great ideas."

Miss Parker had nodded after that. "You have a gift for problem solving," she said quietly. I think she even winked, but maybe she just had something stuck in her eye.

Now I told Tomkin all about my club idea.

"I have a lot of good ideas, Goat," I told Tomkin. "Do you know what the other Tomkin's ideas are?"

Tomkin the Goat yawned and then rammed his head into a fence post.

"Exactly," I said. "His ideas are terrible. All he talks about is building the playground climbing wall and how he's so terrific at soccer. That's it. Think he cares about making clubs or saving turtles or being a good leader? Course not. Tomkin the Human only cares about hanging more goat-napping posters and his own jerkface."

"Baa!" Tomkin the Goat said.

"Good point." I nodded. "Presidents shouldn't call their opponents names. It's beneath them."

Tomkin rumbled and snagged a piece of hair. He made another moaning sound right in my ear.

"All right! All right, Tomkin. I get it. I have a gift for problem solving. I'll go talk to April."

❖ ❖ ❖

April was in her front yard practicing some of her karate moves, her leg making super quick roundhouse kicks low and then high over her head again and again.

Maybe we should come back later, my thought maker supplied. But leaders—heroes—take action, right? I went to her instead.

"Hey," I said.

"Hey." April kept right on kicking.

"Just wanted to say that you're right. I was whining and being awful."

"I know." April kept on kicking.

"I'm having a sleepover tomorrow night with Amanda. Do you want to come? Grandma's going to make some of her famous popcorn."

April's kicks slowed a moment. "Nutella and melted chocolate?"

"Yeah, the good stuff, too. She got Hershey bars." I crossed my legs and sat down on the grass. "Mom could pick you up after we get Amanda?"

April kicked once more and then sat down across from me. "I'll walk over. Are you sure you want me to come? I was kind of mean."

I smiled. "I'm sure. April, can you tell me more about your school? What it's like to be president?"

April leaned back on her elbows. "Are you looking for tips?"

"Maybe," I shrugged. "But I also just want to know how you're doing."

April grabbed a handful of grass and let it trickle through her fingers. "I like the new school, and being president is cool—even if there are only a few kids in my class. But I miss you guys."

"I miss you, too. A lot."

April hopped to her feet. "Want to skip-race to the park?"

I jumped up, too. "Mind if I just run-race instead of skip-racing? I'm still recovering from a recent skip-ping-related malady." My poor bum. I patted it gently.

"Malady?" April tilted her head.

"It's on my vocab list this week." Along with epic, quest, behemoth, requiem, gladiator, and a bunch of other superhero words, thanks to Miss Parker.

Saturday morning, Mom and I went to Amanda's house to pick her up for the sleepover. "Are you sure this is it?" she asked as she pulled into the driveway. A beat-up old shed in the backyard had a huge poster with the outline of a person on it. All around it were a bunch of different sized knives stuck into the wood. The house, old and gray with a sagging front porch, looked about as well cared for as the shed. Snapping in the breeze from the top of the house was a pirate flag, skull and crossbones.

I checked the house number on the mailbox against the text from Amanda. "Yep, this is it."

Mom grabbed my arm as I opened the door to hop out and get Amanda. "What exactly does Mr. Frankston do for a living?"

"Pirate," I said.

"Excuse me?" Mom said, but the word morphed into a scream when her car door was opened.

Standing beside the car was a super tall, incredibly hairy man with a red bandana tied around his head and a mustache curling up on the sides of his mouth. "Arr!" he said. "You must be the Family Beaner!" He bowed deeply, swaying his hands out to the side as he did.

"Um, yes," Mom said and turned off the ignition.

Mr. Frankston stepped back as Mom got out of the car. "I'm, um, Carrie, and this is Lucy."

"Shiver me timbers, it's good to meet the famous Lucy in person." Mr. Frankston winked at me and I noticed he was wearing black eyeliner. "M'lady," he said and bowed again.

I wasn't sure what to do so I kind of bowed and curtsied at once.

"Dad," Amanda almost-growled. "Enough already. The Festival isn't for another month." Amanda slung a duffel bag into the backseat. "Dad's a method actor," she said to Mom, "getting in character to be Hank, the Sword Swallowing, Sword Throwing Pirate in the Ye Olde Time Festival this fall."

"Arr! I feel like it's my maiden voyage all over again. Been in the doldrums these past ten years, a landlubber away from the Festival. But now? I've got fire in the hole!" Mr. Frankston winked at Mom.

"Fire in the what?" I whispered to Amanda, who just rolled her eyes.

"Want to meet my parrot, lassies?" Mr. Frankston said.

"No one wants to meet Chuckles. And he's a parakeet." Amanda rolled her eyes again.

"Avast ye! His name is Blackbeard," Mr. Frankston boomed, "and he be a noble bird."

"You got him on Craigslist. All he says is 'toast.' And you know I hate toast!"

"Lovely to meet you, um, Hank," Mom said. "What time would you like us to bring Amanda back in the morning?"

"I'll be spending the day swabbing the decks," Mr. Frankston said and then squinted up at the sun. "Mayhaps about mid o' the day?"

"Sure, we'll bring her home at noon." Mom sat back in the car and jerked her head to the side to indicate I should do the same.

"But I want to meet Chuckles."

"Later," Mom hissed. "Nice to meet you," she said again to Mr. Frankston.

"Arr! Keep a weather eye open, matey!" Mr. Frankston saluted us and bowed again.

"Is he always Pirate Hank?" I asked Amanda as Mom backed out of the driveway.

"For six months now." Amanda glared out the window. "I hate the sea."

"Can he really swallow swords?"

Amanda shrugged. "It's not that big of deal. The only times he gets nervous about it is when the blades are on fire."

"What?" I asked. "Next time, let's have a sleepover at your house."

"No," Mom and Amanda said at the same time. Mom's face turned bright red. I don't think she meant to say that out loud, not that Amanda noticed.

"Has your dad always been an actor?"

Amanda shifted a little. "Yeah, I guess. He did handyman work for the past few years. But before that, he was a sword thrower. That's how he met Flora the Fortune-Teller, before she ran off with Charlie the funnel cake maker."

"Flora the Fortune-Teller?" Mom echoed.

"My mother." Amanda glared out the window. "I wonder if she predicted she'd leave me when I was still a baby."

Mom's mouth flopped open and shut a couple times. She swallowed like a gobstopper was stuck in her throat. "That must be hard on you," she finally said.

Amanda shrugged.

Mom cleared her throat. "Well, if you'd ever like to talk—"

"Oh boy," I whispered at the same time that Amanda said, "What's in the basket under the sink?"

The car jerked to the right as Mom twisted to face me.

"Weather eye open, matey!" I screeched.

Mom straightened the car but her knuckles turned white as she gripped the wheel. "I'm not sure that question is appropriate for me to answer."

Amanda leaned forward and squeezed Mom's shoulder. "Listen, Mrs. Beaner. I have a pirate as a father. The most he'll say about puberty is 'dead men tell no tales.' My mom's a turtle. I've got questions."

"Well, okay, then," Mom said. She glanced toward me. "What time is April coming over?"

"In an hour. Plenty of time for the two of you to talk." I smiled sweetly at her.

"You were in on this?" she hissed.

"I've got a gift for problem solving."

❖ ❖ ❖

Much later that night, as April and I lay side by side in our sleeping bags on the living room floor, with Amanda snoring on the couch above us, April asked, "How is the race going?"

I shrugged before realizing April couldn't see me in the dark. "It's okay." I told her about my idea for having after-school clubs. "Maybe they could run for, I don't know, three months each and then you could switch to another one. And if everyone met in the cafeteria, it wouldn't take too many teachers to supervise. Plus I think parents could help out, too, if they wanted to."

April rolled to her side and I could sort of see her

face from the hallway light Mom and Dad kept on all night. "What about the turtles?"

"I have an idea for that, for a way to have a new playground and protect them, but I have to work out the details."

"What else?"

I felt a little dumb saying my next idea, but it was easier to do in the dark and to April, who wasn't in the school anymore. "Bravery."

"A what?" April repeated.

"I'm—I'm not very brave," I whispered. "I see people who are, people like Sam and like you. And I want to be brave, too. I was thinking, there are a lot of brave people right here in Autumn Grove. Like the ambulance drivers who didn't even blink when Sam was hurt. They just rushed out and helped him. Like the way Miss Parker saw Tom being mean—saw me being mean, too—and just stopped us, just told us to 'fix it.' Like the police officer who figured out the bike thief was part of a ring of thieves. And the person who comes to our house every week to work with Molly and tell us what she can do and how we can help her. All of those things would be hard for me, but they seem easy to them. Brave. I want to start a hero program, maybe? Something that brings people like that to the school and shows . . ."

But when I glanced over at April, she was asleep, too.

Chapter Fifteen

By Friday, almost a full week after the sleepover, I was finally able to get the answers to some of Amanda's device-related questions out of my head. Even though I had told Mom that Amanda wanted to have a private conversation, she had insisted I sit at the table while they talked. "Once and done," she had said.

I shuddered as I headed into the locker room for gym class.

Ms. Drake spotted me in the hallway. "Lucy!" she called. "A word."

"Narwhal!" I offered.

Ms. Drake's pointy shoulders rose and fell with a sigh. "I'd like to have a word," she said again.

"Applesauce?" I tried. "Magenta!"

Ms. Drake pursed her lips for a moment. "I'd like to *talk* with you about something."

"Oh," I said. "Okay."

We stepped to the side so other girls could make their way into the locker room. Becky was last in line, and I shifted a little away from her. But, just like I knew she would, Becky leaned in with her nosy ears. That kind of made me smile, thinking about ears having noses, but the strict look on Ms. Drake's face wiped the smile away. Then I pictured myself with smiles and noses on my ears, but only for a second.

"Lucy, you have to choose a vice president. The debate and election is Monday. It wouldn't be fair for you to appoint a vice president after the election, not giving the student voters an opportunity to make a fully educated choice."

"But I don't have anyone to be vice president," I pointed out.

"You need to find someone. Try to give me a name by the end of the day." Ms. Drake squeezed my shoulder and strode away.

I slumped into the locker room. My last day as a would-be president. No way would I find someone willing to be my VP. Suddenly, a hand shot out and grabbed my wrist, yanking me into a corner of the locker room. Becky stood in front of me with her eyes sliding from side to side in the locker room, making sure no one would see her talking to me. "I'm willing to do the job."

"Why in the world would I want you to be my vice president?" I asked. "I don't like you all that much."

"*No one* likes you all that much, Lucy, that's the problem." Becky rolled her eyes. "But if you're president, than I'm sure you'd be popular. Everyone would want to talk with you. I've heard you talking to people at recess and at lunch, and Lily told me you convinced about half your class to be pro-turtle during a class debate." She fluffed her hair and shifted to her other hip. "*And* I know you're able to be pretty convincing when you want to be." She leaned in and lowered her voice, "Penny loafers, remember?"

I did. Way back at the beginning of last year when Becky and I were best friends, I had shown up to school in penny loafers. A couple people called them grandma shoes, but I talked a lot (repeating Mom's lines) about how they're great quality and would last forever and always be stylish. Wouldn't you know it, Becky showed up in penny loafers the next day. And now April wears them every day.

But I also remembered when Becky stopped wearing them. It was the day after Molly was born, and I had spent the day at home with my new family unit. At school the next day, Tomkin the Human broke up with me (I shuddered as I remembered kissing his raw chicken lips). And that's the day Becky retired her penny loafers, knowing my days of being popular—and her friend—were over.

At the end of fourth grade, we kind of, sort of had made up, but we never would be good friends again. That didn't mean we couldn't be co-candidates. Becky was always and forever going to be looking for ways to become more popular. But maybe that also meant she'd figure out how to give me an actual chance at winning this election.

"If I did make you my VP, it wouldn't mean we're friends again," I said.

"Of course not. But I think together we've got a shot."

"If you do anything mean, you're out."

Becky rolled her eyes. "Fine. You try not to do anything weird."

"Weird? Like what?"

Becky cocked an eyebrow.

"Oh, yeah. Like goat-napping."

"Yes, like goat-napping. Or splitting your skirt in the middle of class. Or howling like a dying dog. Or—"

"Got it! Got it. Okay." I put my hand out to shake. She squeezed my hand hard, making the little bones rub together. I squeezed hers back until both of our knuckles were white and the skin stretched out around them.

Just then, a group of girls came into our corner of the locker room and Becky erupted in giggles. She nudged me and made her eyes go wide as marbles. Catching on, I started to laugh, too, but it sounded more like a cat choking on a drink of water.

"Oh, Lucy, you're *so funny*!" Becky put her arm around me. "I can't believe you said that!"

"Me, either!" I said, since I hadn't said anything.

"And I *love* your idea about clubs!" Becky turned to the group. "Hey, Bree." She beckoned to one of the girls, a fifth grader I hadn't met before. "Lucy was just talking about her club idea. She was saying that maybe we could start a musical club."

Bree's bottom lip popped out. "Are you serious?"

"Um."

"What's your favorite *Hamilton* track?" Bree asked.

Thank you, Mom, for playing the *Hamilton* soundtrack over and over and over! "Right Hand Man."

"Speaking of which," Becky said, "Lucy's just asked me to be her right-hand person. I'm going to be vice president!"

"Satisfied." Bree nodded. As she went to her locker, she and the other girls whistled another song from the musical.

Becky leaned in. "One group down."

❖ ❖ ❖

Becky caught up with me at the end of the day. "Listen," she said and grabbed my backpack to slow me down. She was wearing platform sandals with enormous wedge heels and stumbled behind me.

"If you had proper footwear, you'd be able to keep up," I told her but slowed.

"I wanted to talk with you about that," Becky huffed. "Up your style game."

I glanced down at what I was wearing—a red T-shirt, orange shorts, and gym sneakers. "What's wrong with what I'm wearing?"

Becky shook her head. "Not very presidential."

"Seriously? They're just clothes. They don't matter."

"Have you ever been president? I didn't think so." Becky gestured at her flowy white dress. "Try something more like this. Or at the very least, something that actually matches. Maybe brush your hair? People like people who look like they care what they look like."

It took me about a full minute to translate that sentence in my head. "I don't want people to vote for me based on what I look like."

"Obviously." Becky crossed her arms. "But you do want them to vote for you, don't you? They're not even going to listen to what you say when you look like you pulled some clothes out from under your bed and shoved them onto your body before you ever open your eyes in the morning."

"How did—"

"We used to have sleepovers, remember?" Becky pushed her hair back from her face. "Just think about it, please."

I ran my fingers through my hair, trying to straighten it a little, and headed toward my bus line. Sam was waiting there. Bree had been talking to him and gestured toward me with her thumb before walking away. "Is it true?" His eyes weren't crinkly at all and his mouth was a straight line.

"Hey, Sam," I said. "Is what true?"

"Bree said Becky's going to be your vice president. After everything she's done to you, you wouldn't be that dumb, right?"

I shrugged. "Not exactly a line for the job."

Sam shook his head. "Are you that desperate to win?"

"I'm not desperate," I said. "I just want to win."

"Why?" Sam glared at me.

"Because I think I have good ideas, for clubs *and* for the turtles. I want to help. I've been thinking a lot about the turtle thing and what if we—"

"Whatever." Sam turned away.

"Just listen to me, please!" I grabbed his arm to stop him. I did it without thinking. I didn't mean to grab *that* arm. I mean, the giant red cast should've been pretty obvious. I know that, but somehow that's exactly what I did. I grabbed at his broken arm. Thankfully, Sam dodged out of the way before I could actually touch it. Still, I gasped at my own self and then covered my mouth with my hands. "I'm so sorry! I'm so sorry!"

Sam's jaw set as he turned toward me. "Don't you ever get tired of apologizing all the time, Lucy?"

"Sam, if you'd just stop and let me talk with you . . ." I lowered my hands and stepped toward him. If I could just tell him about my ideas for president, about how I wanted to do the right thing, about how it wasn't to hurt him. I took a deep breath, realizing he was about to storm off. "I told you I was sorry about the vice president thing." He winced, but I kept going anyway. "Me running for president doesn't have anything to do with you or Sheldon. It's about me!"

"Of course it's about you. It's always about you."

This time I winced. That's not really the word for the face I made. It was more like if he had slapped me. It took me a second to breathe again, like my face was still bracing for impact. The thing is, I knew he was right. I did make everything about me. Or at least, I used to be that selfish and maybe part of me always would be. But I was trying. And wanting to be president wasn't selfish. I wasn't running because I wanted to be popular or to have a lot of attention. Maybe that's what old Lucy used to be like. But now, I was running because I thought I could make a difference. Because I wanted to make up for all the times I had been selfish. When I could suck in air again, I tried to tell him that. "Sam, that's not fair—"

"Who cares about fair?" Sam yelled. I mean it, he yelled. And not just by Sam standards of talking, where a regular voice felt like a yell because he usually spoke softly or not at all. This was a real yell, one that made a vein I had never seen before pop out the middle of his forehead, taking so much force his arms flailed out, making his chest rise and then fall, and causing me to wince away from him all over again. "What makes you deserve fairness? I sure didn't." He raised his casted arm again. "You're not being fair to *me*."

"Sam," I whispered, since just standing there and not running away from him took all my energy and there wasn't enough left to talk normally, "you don't even *want* to be president. I know you don't."

Sam's eyes met mine and it felt worse than if he had yelled again. His eyes were so angry, so full of pain, so disappointed, so . . . much. "You don't know how I feel." His voice was quiet again but echoed in my ears like a scream anyway.

"Maybe you could tell me, then," I said, forcing myself to look right into those eyes even though they didn't belong on Sam's face.

He blinked and opened his mouth and I thought maybe, maybe everything would be okay. But that's when Becky showed up, her fake giggly laugh zipping between me and Sam. She threw her arm around my shoulder. "Listen, prez," she said too loudly. "I've been thinking more about our campaign. Can I come over later?"

Becky grabbed my shoulder and turned me away from Sam and toward a group of kids behind us. "We're going to have so much fun!"

"Stop!" I said and shrugged out from under her grasp. "I need to talk to Sam."

But when I turned back around, Sam was disappearing behind his bus door.

Chapter Sixteen

Dad answered the door wearing his apron when Becky arrived at home an hour later. "Becky," he said and nodded.

"Hi, Mr. Beaner! How are you?" She giggled, even though no one had said anything funny. "What's that delicious smell?"

The smell was not delicious. Dad had been working on one of his DDs (Daddy's Delights—a made-up dinner recipe that would either be amazing or disgusting or maybe a little of both) when I told him Becky was going to come over to help with the campaign. When I mentioned that she was going to be my vice president, he made me watch all of these YouTube videos of a man named Dick Cheney and forgot about the brussels sprouts, chicken, and cranberry medley in the oven. Only one thing smells worse than cooked brussels sprouts, and that's charred brussels sprouts with shriveled up cranberries and dried-out chicken. I told Dad it smelled like fried farts and onions. Dad said it smelled like politics and oppression.

But he didn't answer Becky—I guess despite his "choose to be happy" and "always forgive" talk, he still was a little grouchy with her about the whole only-your-friend-in-secret bullying from last year. He just opened the door a little wider. "Amanda!" he called out, way too happy.

"Amanda's here?" I shot up from the kitchen table and ran to the front door.

"What's *she* doing here?" both Becky and Amanda said at the same time.

"Becky's helping with my campaign," I answered Amanda first.

"I'm going to be vice president! I hope you'll consider voting for us," Becky trilled.

"No."

"Excuse me?" Becky said as my father the traitor laughed.

"No, I won't consider it. I don't like you. I'm voting for Sheldon and Sam."

"You mean Sam and Sheldon." Becky crossed her arms.

Amanda's nostrils flared but she didn't answer Becky. "Is your mom home yet?" she asked me.

I blinked at Amanda. "Um, she'll be home in a couple minutes."

"Cool." Amanda walked past me and plopped on the couch.

"Are you here to hang out with my mom?" I asked.

"We have plans." Amanda kicked off her sneakers and picked up the remote, clicking on the television.

"You have plans . . . with *my mom*?"

"Yeah." Amanda tossed her water bottle, making it flip twice in the air before landing on the base. Molly, lying on a blanket on the other side of the living room, gurgled and waved her arms in the air. Amanda grinned at her and did it again, making Molly laugh when she landed another flip.

I bit my lip, thinking. At the sleepover, April and I had spent most of the time watching movies, eating popcorn, and helping Grandma plan her wedding (she was against the whole white dress thing but said she'd consider putting flowers in her hair). Even after I had escaped into the living room, Amanda had hung out a lot with Mom in the kitchen, asking all sorts of questions.

"Would you like to stay for dinner, Amanda?" Dad called from the kitchen.

Amanda sniffed the air and winced. "No thanks. Mrs. Beaner and I will grab something at the mall."

"What?" I gasped.

"At the mall." Amanda changed to the nature channel. "Do you have a soda or something?"

"No." I shook my head. "You have your water bottle."

"Yeah, but that's for flipping, not drinking." She tilted it to the side and sloshed the water. "I have it to the perfect bottle-flipping level."

Becky crossed her arms. "Isn't bottle flipping *so* last year?"

"Aren't you?" Amanda replied.

"How about milk or Gatorade?" Dad said, as if any of what was happening was normal.

"Nah, that's cool, Mr. Beaner. I'm not a fan of anything squeezed out of an udder, or of salty water."

"Understandable, Amanda."

"I'll take a—" But Becky didn't bother finishing when Dad strode back into the kitchen. "Do your friends usually come over to see your mom?" Becky asked. She still stood in the doorway.

"I don't know," I answered honestly. Because maybe they did. Maybe this was, like, a thing, Mom taking my friends to the mall.

Mom's car pulled into the driveway. I stayed by the front door with Becky standing just behind me as Mom came into the house.

Mom kissed me on the cheek as she walked in. "Becky," Mom said with wide eyes. "I haven't seen you in quite some time."

"Hello, Mrs. Beaner," Becky said in her sugary talking-to-adults voice. "How are you this—"

But Mom had spotted Amanda by then and exclaimed, "Amanda! I'm so happy to see you!"

"Hey, Mrs. Beaner." Amanda sat up and squished her feet back into her sneakers. "You ready to go? I told Mr. Beaner we'd grab dinner at the mall." She waved a hand under her nose.

Mom sniffed. "Yeah, that sounds great, Amanda. Let me just get changed and I'll be ready to go."

I trailed Mom down the hall to her bedroom. "Are you seriously taking Amanda to the mall?"

"Yes, she said she needed a little help finding clothes that she likes." Mom shrugged.

"But you're going without *me*?"

Mom smiled over her shoulder. "You hate the mall, Lucy. Every time we go, all you want is a soft pretzel and quarters for the arcade. You never want to actually shop." She pushed her hair out of her face. "I should've mentioned it to you. We made plans while we were talking at your sleepover, and you and April were in the other room. I'm sorry. Honestly, I sort of forgot until just now. Does this bother you?"

You know what? I almost said something stupid. Something like *but Amanda's* my *friend*. And then I reminded myself that I was done being selfish. Amanda didn't have anyone else to go shopping with and Mom loved going shopping. This didn't have anything to do with me, unless I made it about me. So instead, I said, "I think it's cool."

Mom stilled, a statue for a moment. "Excuse me?"

"Cool," I said. "Have a great time."

I turned and walked smack into Becky. "Mrs. Beaner, could you pick up some presidential clothes for Lucy?"

This time I was the one saying, "Excuse me?"

Becky sidestepped me. "Most of her clothes are . . ."

Mom turned, and both she and Becky looked up and down at my outfit. "What?" I licked my thumb and rubbed at a splotch of jelly on my T-shirt from breakfast.

"I'll see what I can do," Mom replied.

"Great!" Becky bounced a little. I forgot how much she bounced. "Now that your look is taken care of, we can address the next biggest hurdle."

"Hurdle?" I asked. Giving up on rubbing out the splotch, I pulled up the hem of my shirt and tried to suck out the stain.

Becky raised her eyebrow. "The candidate assembly is Monday."

"Right. I've been working on the speech. And I think the debate part will be okay." I shrugged. "I actually have a lot of ideas. Listen, I think—"

Becky held up her hand like a stop sign. "No one's going to care about the speech. What they care about is the *person*. That's what we have to work on."

"But I'm *me*."

"Exactly." Becky nibbled on her lip, then said, "You know Tom is going to lead with how he's a soccer star, and Sam's going to be playing the hero card. You've got to do something between now and then that's just as awesome."

"So you want me to suddenly be great at sports?"

Amanda, still waiting for Mom to change, laughed. "Sort of like archery?" Which was totally not cool to bring up. At Camp Paleo, I had thought maybe archery was my awesome. But I ended up hitting other teams' targets and scaring Mr. Bosserman. I mean, Gaga.

"Yeah, maybe not sports." Becky crossed her arms and stared at me. "But maybe you could do something like Sam."

"Sure, I'll just go right out and save some toddlers. No sweat." I rolled my eyes.

Becky sighed. "Well, maybe you could do something *similar*. Something . . ."

"Heroic," I whispered.

"Yes! Be a hero," Becky suggested. "By Monday."

❖ ❖ ❖

By Saturday, I still hadn't become a sports prodigy or saved the city.

We do not have to be heroes overnight. That's what Eleanor Roosevelt said. Well, sorry to prove you wrong, First Lady. But I had just one more day to become heroic.

Even though it was nearly October, the sky was as bright blue and sunshiny warm as any day in August when I woke up that Sunday. Mom said we had to take advantage of the weather while we could, so Dad had packed lunches, I gathered sand toys for Molly, and Mom smeared all of us with sunscreen. Then we hit the road for Laurel Lake. Maybe I'd find a kitten to save along the way. April had a karate tournament nearby at two o'clock and Mom and Dad promised we'd be back by then. We always made sure we were home by one o'clock, when Molly had nap time. Otherwise, she became a werebaby.

"Do you want to ask any of the pack to come along?" Mom asked as she loaded up the car.

I shook my head.

"Everything okay there?" Mom closed the trunk and pulled me against her side. She squeezed my shoulder.

I nodded.

"It's just, you're not actually talking," Mom laughed. She squeezed again. "Is it all right with you that I'm spending time with Amanda? If it isn't, or if you feel awkward or left out about it, we should talk."

I looked up at Mom and made my face smile. "It's not a problem at all." It was the truth. I'm glad Amanda had my mom.

But I couldn't stop thinking about the fact that tomorrow, I'd have to stand in front of the school, next to Tom and Sam, and somehow convince the whole school I was likable and a leader. Why was I doing this? It'd be so much easier to just back out. But every time I thought I didn't have a chance and should just quit, I thought about Kyle nodding in the cafeteria when I talked about clubs; I thought about the kids being pro-turtle in the classroom because I had convinced them; I thought about Tom being in charge and not caring about anyone but Tom.

"Worried about the debates tomorrow?" Dad asked. I hadn't realized he was standing just behind Mom.

I nodded again.

"And then the elections are right after, right?"

"Yeah," I said. "I'm not going to win."

"Don't say that, Lucy," Dad cut in. "You can't go into those types of things with your head down. You'll have lost before you've ever begun."

Mom propped my chin up with her fingertips. I watched her face shift, knowing she was sifting through her thoughts. She's really good at doing that, figuring out which words to use and listening to them inside before letting them loose. Me? I tend to open my mouth and barf out thoughts before they're even totally formed. Her face settled, her mouth soft but unsmiling, and her eyes steady and kind. "You might lose," she said, her fingers keeping my face upturned toward hers even though I tried to look away. "You might. But you're sharing what's important to you and you're standing up for yourself and your classmates. The results won't change that."

I swallowed and nodded. Mom kissed my forehead. "Sometimes even when you think you're losing, you discover you've actually won."

"But I really want to win," I heard myself saying.

Mom squeezed me against her. "I know."

❖ ❖ ❖

As soon as we hit the beach, I ran straight toward the water. Laurel Lake was huge, but not so big that I couldn't see the other side of it. Tall pine trees shot up all around the water's edge, and the water itself was the color of the evergreen needles. Maybe that was from the reflection of the trees, or maybe it was from the soft green sludge that coated the bottom of the lake. I chose to think it was the reflection. A couple weeks before school had started, Mom and Dad had taken Sam and me to Laurel Lake for the day. I swam until my fingers were wrinkled and when I had left the water, my hair was green, too, from all of the slimy seaweed. I had gathered it up and thrown it like a baseball at Sam, who had swatted it back to land with a plop in front of me.

This time, Mom had said not to bother bringing a swimsuit. I had put on one under my clothes, just in case. But Mom was right. The water was so cold, when it covered my feet, I swear I could feel each and every little bone shudder and turn to icicles. I yelped and ran back to our blanket. Mom was trying to lower Molly onto the sand but every time Molly's feet got close to the sand, she'd lift her legs up and away, like when I try to make the opposite ends of a magnet collide. Mom laughed so hard I could see her ribs stretching under her T-shirt.

Mom finally gave up on Mollsters and put her on the blanket instead. It felt strange to be at the lake with barely anyone other than us. A few yards away, there was another blanket with a couple on it reading books, but other than that, we were the only ones around. It felt like we were at a private beach. And maybe a little lonely. Maybe I should've asked Sam to come along. Not that he would've. He and Sheldon were probably rehearsing for the debates.

"Maybe we'll soak up some sun and then go for a hike?" Dad asked.

"Yes!" I shouted. Laurel Lake had a path around the side that led to a little mountainside I could climb up. Giant boulders with perfect little pockets for my fingers. At the top, if I squinted, I could see my house. I mean, maybe it was my house. It had a roof like mine.

But after a few minutes of sun soaking in a beach chair, Dad's breath seeped out of his chest like a deflating balloon and I knew his eyes were closed behind his sunglasses. I went to nudge him, but Mom stopped me. "Let him rest a little. He was up with Molly a lot last night."

Molly was sitting up with Mom just behind her. When my baby sister got tired of sitting, she'd just flop back. She smiled and tried to eat the little bucket she held.

"Mind if I go for a walk myself?" I asked.

Mom bit her lip, considering. "You're going to stay out of the water, right?"

I shivered. "Of course!"

"Just along the shoreline, okay? No trying to climb the boulders yourself. And bring your phone!"

I nabbed my phone off the towel and headed down to the shoreline. A walk would be perfect for figuring out how to organize my speech. If only it also would give me a way to suddenly become a hero!

I thought more about the bravery program. I had no idea if it'd actually work, but maybe it would. I already knew a bunch of heroes. I bet everyone else did, too. If everyone suggested a hero they knew, and some of those heroes were able to come in and meet with students, we'd learn so much about being brave.

Chapter Seventeen

We left Laurel Lake a couple hours later, just in time for Molly's werebaby-prevention nap and for me to get showered and ready to go to April's karate tournament. Dad dropped me off outside the high school where the tournament was taking place. "You sure you're okay by yourself?"

I nodded. "My friends are all inside."

"You seem a little down. Everything okay?"

I shrugged. I wasn't going to become a hero by Monday morning, especially not at a karate tournament. With a building full of budding ninjas, I didn't stand a chance at coming to anyone's rescue.

And maybe a big part of me was worried about what I had just said to Dad: that my friends were all inside. Were they still my friends?

"Do you know any heroes?" I asked Dad.

"Of course," Dad said. "Your mom's a hero."

I rolled my eyes. "I mean, for real."

"I'm serious." Dad smiled. "She makes every day special. She gives with her whole heart all the time. She sees things in ways I never would've without her. And she's raising amazing daughters who are just like her."

I smiled. "Thanks, Dad."

"Now, go cheer on your friend."

I nodded, readjusting my thoughts as I did. I was right back to doing what had made Sam and April so angry—making everything about me. The tournament was about April. I kissed Dad's cheek and left the car.

❖ ❖ ❖

I was a little nervous about finding my pack in the crowded gymnasium. We'd gone to past tournaments to cheer on April, so I knew the gym would be divvied up into a dozen or so matted rings. I also knew that we might have a long wait until it was April's turn to fight. But I didn't need to worry; I spotted Sheldon immediately.

Sheldon would've been impossible to miss, and not just because he was chanting "Save the Shelled Ones!"

just inside the gym lobby. There also was the fact that he wore a huge papier-mâché green turtle head like it was a hat and an all-green sweat suit with a giant shell made out of the same material as the hat (only painted brown), which covered his back like a backpack. People kept snapping his picture with their phones or taking selfies with him. "Smile!" a mom said as her kids crowded around Sheldon.

"The destruction of reptilian habitat is nothing to smile about," Sheldon said.

Sheldon pushed a pamphlet detailing how the new playground was set to begin construction in a couple weeks right over the turtle habitat into my hand. Already he had spread out a bunch of green T-shirts with *Save the Shelled Ones* printed across the front. A sign next to them said the shirts were ten bucks each, with all of the money going toward "Sam and Sheldon Campaign to Save the Turtles."

"Is Sam here?" I asked. Sheldon tossed one of the T-shirts my way. For a second, I hesitated. Putting it on was sort of endorsing the competition, right? But then I just pulled it over my head anyway.

Sheldon posed for a picture before turning toward me, the smile dissolving from his face. "I'm more worried about Amanda! She was supposed to be here an hour ago."

I pulled my phone out of my pocket. "Did you text her?"

"I can't reach . . ." Sheldon twisted, but his face kept disappearing into his turtle head mask and the giant shell shifted so he couldn't bend his arms. He twisted back, his face red and sweaty. I wondered how much the hat and backpack weighed. "It's like I have T-Rex arms!"

I hit send on a text to Amanda and heard the ding just behind me. In front of me, Sheldon's red face somehow flamed even more. I turned slowly around and there was Amanda. But not Amanda. She was so pretty. I had seen Amanda dressed up before, when we had a "dance" at Camp Paleo. (She and Sheldon were the only ones who had danced; the rest of us just sort of swayed around the edges of the room and drank too much watery punch, considering the lack of plumbing on the campgrounds.)

The Amanda in front of me wasn't wearing her usual mesh shorts and black T-shirt. Her hair wasn't in its usual frizzy helmet around her head. Her face wasn't scowling and pale. Instead, Amanda's dark hair was shiny and smooth, parted down the middle and laying in soft layers. It made her face look less moon-shaped, or maybe that was the lip gloss that added a glimmer to her mouth and maybe she was even wearing a little more makeup, but if so, it was so soft and light I couldn't be sure. Maybe it wasn't makeup. I squinted to narrow in on Amanda's eyes. Something was definitely different there. Her eyebrows! She had two distinct eyebrows now instead of one that thinned a little before running into the second.

Amanda wore a long cobalt-blue cardigan over blue leggings covered in tiny green turtles. When Mom and Amanda had gotten home after the shopping trip, I had asked Mom how it had been. "Epic," she had said. Now I saw why.

"What do you think?" Amanda asked.

I glanced back at Sheldon; his eyes were huge as he took in Amanda. "You look amazing!"

Amanda smiled; she didn't do that often enough. It brightened her whole face and seemed to shine through her eyes. "You, too," she answered Sheldon. They smiled at each other just long enough to make me feel squirmy. Finally, Amanda squeezed behind the table, and Sheldon, his face split in a grin, went back to pushing pamphlets.

Tons of trophies lined a banquet table on the other side of the lobby. They looked like gilded shark teeth, row after row after row from tallest to shortest. A boy stood in front of them with a mess of brown curls. *Sam!* I thought, before remembering that he didn't like me anymore. Sam turned a little and I could see the side of his face. He stared at the trophies. "I'll be right back, Amanda," I said as I shuffled out from behind the crowded table and past turtle Sheldon.

I didn't know what to do, even though I had rushed over like I had a plan. *Come on, thought maker, come up with a plan!* Nothing. My whole brain was filled with one image, and it was the mantle at Sam's house, crowded with trophies and ribbons and pictures of him being awesome. And suddenly, I was slipping my hand into Sam's good hand. Sam's head whipped to the side and I knew he was looking at me, but I kept my eyes on the trophies. I squeezed and for just a second, he let our hands drop to his side. Sam sighed. He squeezed my hand. Then we both turned and walked in opposite directions. He headed toward Sheldon and Amanda, and I went into the gymnasium to look for April.

❖ ❖ ❖

I spotted April quickly in the crowded gymnasium. Or, rather, I spotted her family. They were hard to miss, with April's littlest brother jumping on a bleacher plank and with her teenage sister's hands outstretched on either side but looking at her phone on her lap instead of the toddler. Her second to youngest brother, Simon, was snoring, spread out like a wet noodle with his head resting on one bleacher, his back against a second and his legs dangling over a third. April's mother was pulling bagged lunches out of an enormous diaper bag. Her father was braiding April's hair into two tight pigtails. And Scrappy was on the gym floor in front of the bleachers, mimicking the moves of a black belt who was going through a bō staff routine on the mat in front of him.

Scrappy kept missing moves and ended up twisting around, kicking out, jabbing with his arm, and falling into a crumpled heap. I clapped for him anyway as I walked up. "You look like all you need is a light saber."

"Thanks, Lucy!" He wiped his brow and tucked his imaginary light saber into his back pocket (which also was imaginary since he was wearing sweat pants).

"Hey, you called me Lucy. Usually you call me April's friend."

Scrappy shrugged. "It's time to move on."

"Scrappy!" Mrs. Chester beckoned. "Come sit down! The match is about to start." April's dad finished with the braid just as someone on the loudspeaker called out for all fighters to take to the mat.

"You should've been here earlier, Luce," Scrappy said. *Luce?*

"Why?" I settled into the seat next to him. His mouth twitched a little.

"Someone in a wheelchair did this." He went from seated to launching upward with his arm scissoring outward.

"Watch it!" April's sister snapped and ducked to miss his flailing arm.

Scrappy ignored her, his face serious and eyes huge. "But still in his wheelchair! And he knocked this other boy and *kapow*! That boy's helmet? The fake glass part just went *pow*!" His fisted hands flew open, with his fingers waggling.

"Wow," I said.

"Yeah. You can say that again. Wow. I bet it was so cool to see."

"You didn't see it?"

"No," Scrappy said. "I just heard about it."

Mrs. Chester leaned forward, her eyes on the mat. April shoved on her helmet. I thought about texting Sam, letting him know he was about to miss her first fight, but just then he strode into the gymnasium. I waved toward him just as someone called his name three or four rows behind me. I didn't want to be obvious and whip around, but it sounded like Lily.

Sam walked right past me, up to that group. He sort of nodded as he passed but didn't slow down.

Mrs. Chester cupped her hands around her mouth. "Be first, April! First kick, first punch!" April glanced our way and Mrs. Chester held up her pointer finger. April nodded and went back to watching the match before hers. It was a little weird seeing a mom wearing an enormous peace pendant telling her daughter to be the first to kick someone.

"Mama," Scrappy said, and pulled on his mom's arm. "Mama, can I play on your phone? Mama. Mama. Mamamamamamama."

"Scrappy!" Mrs. Chester growled. "Can't you see April's about to take the mat?"

Scrappy sat down again, his arms crossed. Mr. Chester stood. "You've got this, April!" he shouted.

Scrappy pulled his bagged lunch closer just as the match began. Now Mrs. Chester was on her feet, too. The referee whistled and April and the other girl bowed to each other. The other girl was about a half-foot taller than April, but my friend didn't look the least bit intimidated. She launched herself toward the girl, her sidekick hammering outward.

"Yes!" I cheered as April was awarded the first point. The first to get to three won the match.

"What happened?" Scrappy asked.

"If you'd watch, you'd—" But Mrs. Chester's words trickled into a groan as she glanced toward Scrappy. The jam had slipped out between Scrappy's sandwich, sending a giant glob falling. It landed in slow motion, with a wet plop, in the middle of his sleeping brother Simon's forehead. Simon's arms shot out, knocking over Scrappy's water bottle (open of course) and kicking his sister, who startled the baby, who began to wail. Then Simon's hand shot up to the goo on his forehead, shoving it up in a raspberry streak through his hair.

The referee whistled. In all the commotion we missed the next round! The other girl was awarded the point.

"Great! We missed it," Mr. Chester grumbled. "Get control of yourself, buddy. Not everything has to be about you!"

"But I can't *see*," Scrappy whined.

"Not this again!" Mrs. Chester shook her head. She patted the baby's rump until he stopped screaming. "Stand if you need to, but no one is blocking your view. You're just not watching!"

I picked up the water bottle and an apple that had rolled out of Scrappy's lunch bag.

He took them from me and bit the apple with an

angry slurping sound. "Dad!" he said around a second bite. "What's happening? Dad. Dad! What's—"

"Just *watch*," Mr. Chester said.

I was starting to regret sitting with Scrappy. But then he slumped onto the bench, his chubby cheek resting against his hand. "Well," I said, "right now, April is bouncing a little. Whoa, she just lunged forward like she was going to punch but—no way!—it was a fake. And the girl fell for it! She's trying to hit April with a ridge hand." I swiped out my arm so Scrappy could see what that meant. "But—yes!—April landed a roundhouse kick to her other side! April won!" I jumped to my feet and next to me, Scrappy did, too. He held the apple in his mouth by his teeth so he could clap and cheer.

"Thanks!" he said as we settled back down. He gathered up the trash into his lunch bag. "I'm going to throw this away!" he said to Mrs. Chester. Scrappy skipped down the bleachers toward the trash cans. He could've turned right and hit the trash cans a few yards down from where we sat, but instead he turned left, going all the way back to the trash cans we had passed on the way through the doors to the gym. I chewed on my lip, watching him.

"Mrs. Chester," I asked, "has Scrappy ever had to go to the eye doctor?"

She laughed. "No, he sees fine. He's just shorter than you. He always complains about not being able to see at these tournaments."

Scrappy skipped back toward us. "I think he might be serious," I said.

"Really?" Mrs. Chester tilted her head as Scrappy approached. He walked right past where we sat on the bleachers. "Scrappy!" she called and waved her arms. When he finally spotted her and turned back around, Mrs. Chester leaned into Mr. Chester. "Let's make Scrappy an optometrist appointment."

❖ ❖ ❖

After the tournament, the Chesters left. April was crammed in the back of the minivan with a huge trophy for first place in sparring. Amanda's dad pulled up in an orange Jeep with a pirate flag flying from the top to pick her up at the same time that Sheldon's mom swerved to the curb in a brown station wagon. Both parents wore *Save the Shelled Ones* T-shirts.

Amanda's dad yelled, "By the powers! Are ye the lad Sheldon's older sister?"

Sheldon's mom blushed. "I'm his mother. You must be Amanda's father."

"Arr!"

"I've heard so much about you." She put out her hand to shake.

Amanda's dad took her hand and wrapped his other hand around hers, too. "Pleased to meet your acquaintance, matey. Is the Mr. Harris about?" Amanda's dad peered into the car.

"Um, no," she said. "Mr. Harris—Don—is no longer with us. He passed away."

"I'm sorry to hear that," Mr. Frankston said in a regular voice, the pirate act vanishing on the spot. "I had no idea."

Sheldon's mom shook her head and smiled. "Don't be sorry. It was a long time ago, when Sheldon was a toddler."

The pirate act came back in full effect as Sheldon and Amanda got to their cars. "Ahoy, mateys!" Mr. Frankston called as the Jeep pulled away behind the station wagon.

For a few seconds after they all drove away, Sam and I didn't speak. I finally sank down on the curb to wait for my parents. Sam sat down beside me.

A minute or two passed without either of us saying anything.

"Are you nervous about tomorrow?" I finally asked.

"The debate?" Sam's voice was hard. I nodded, but he just shrugged. "Whatever."

"It's just—everyone will be watching us, so I bet it'll be hard for you—"

"I'm not quitting, Lucy, so just stop trying to convince me." He scooted a few inches away.

"I'm not trying to! I just thought we could talk about it? You seem upset and—"

"So what?"

"So maybe if we talk about it . . ."

"Back off, Lucy." Sam jumped to his feet. I did, too. He started to walk away, but I followed, one step behind. Except when Sam whipped around, he knocked into me. "Back off!" he said again. I closed my eyes and didn't move. "Why do you always have to be here, everywhere? Why do you always think *you* have to fix things? You can't fix everything."

I opened my mouth but before I could speak, Sam did. "Can't I just be sad?"

A horn honked and I turned to see Grandma in her giant station wagon waving in my direction. I turned back toward Sam, wanting to tell him *no, you can't just be sad because that makes me sad and I don't want either of us to be that way.* But he was gone.

Chapter Eighteen

"Everything okay with Sam?" Grandma asked as I got into her car.

"No," I moaned. The sunlight hit her diamond ring and just about blinded me. I twisted to stare out the window instead. "Nothing is all right. We have the debate tomorrow."

"Are you worried about going on stage?"

I shrugged. "A little, I guess. I mean, sort of."

Grandma twisted her head back, one caterpillar-sized eyebrow popping up, and then looked back to the road. "Just sort of?"

I bit my lip, then blurted, "We get the first five minutes to just talk, no interruptions."

"Ah," Grandma said. She nodded.

"What?"

"Uninterrupted time to talk sounds nice."

I stared back out the window. "I have a lot of ideas but all anyone wants to talk about is Tomkin the Goat, or the time I split my skirt and all the other stupid stuff I've done."

"So you'll be able to tell them all about your ideas." Grandma's voice was apology soft. I realized she felt sorry for me. I ducked under my T-shirt so she wouldn't see my red face. "And maybe, once they hear from you, they'll vote for you?"

I shrugged again. "Maybe."

"You don't sound confident."

I sighed, and my T-shirt mask rattled. "Tomkin the Human is popular. Sam's a hero. I don't have a shot."

"So why are you running?" Grandma stopped the car. I peeked out and saw she had pulled over to the side of the road. She stared at me. "Those five minutes must be pretty important to you."

I nodded and swallowed down all the itchy thoughts and worries and maybe even hope that were tickling my throat.

"I'm proud of you," Grandma said. "I don't have a lot of regrets in my life. Really, when I think about it, I only have three. And each of those happened because I didn't speak up when I should've."

"Like when?" I prodded.

"Well, when I was your age was one. My neighbor was my best friend. I'd go to her house after school every single day. We loved all the same music, swapped clothes all the time, made up secret stories and acted them out. Best friends, you know?"

I nodded.

"But we had a difference, too. Her skin was brown and mine isn't. That was the biggest difference, but somehow it was one we never talked about. Even when I saw teachers laying into her about things like forgetting a homework assignment even though I had forgotten, too, and was just told to bring it in the next day. Even when the clerk at the candy shop trailed just behind her and never me. Even when we got a little older and I got invited to parties and football games and she didn't."

"But how did you know all those things happened because her skin was brown?" I asked.

Grandma's nostrils flared out with the power of a mega sigh. "I just did. And she did, too. But we never talked about it, and then we drifted apart. It was a big mistake, the not talking, not being heard. It would've been hard to talk about, but I should've."

"Eleanor Roosevelt did that. Talk about racism and

why it was wrong. It got her in trouble. A lot of people didn't like what she had to say. But she talked about it anyway."

"She was an amazing woman."

"Did you know her?"

Grandma swatted the air like my question was a bug. "Did I know her? Toots, I was five years old when she died. How old do you think I am?"

"Let's talk about something else," I said, borrowing a line from Scrappy.

"Did I know her?" Grandma muttered. She turned around and shifted the car into drive, then eased back onto the road. For some reason, it was easier to talk to her when she was facing the other direction.

"Sam's going to have to talk, too." I twisted my fingers in my lap. "Tomorrow, I mean. He's going to have to talk before the debate. And then he's going to have to debate."

Grandma's bottom lip jutted out as she nodded.

"What?" I said again.

"Sam's not much of a public speaker, is he?"

I shook my head.

"And maybe part of you, a small part that isn't worried about Sam, is thinking that maybe if he does a terrible job, you might get his votes?"

I shook my head faster. No way was I thinking that. I wanted my friend to be amazing. I wanted him to be awesome on stage. *I just want to be a little bit better*. Shut it, thought maker! Now's not the time to be a jerk.

"Sam's so sad all the time. I don't want him to be sad."

"That's not up to you." Grandma's eyes met mine for a second in the rearview mirror. I tried not to stare at her diamond ring. "I told you I had three regrets. The second is that I spent too long pretending to feel something I didn't."

"You mean with my grandpa?" I had never met him; he left before Mom was even born. Grandma never talked about him at all.

She nodded, her cheeks wobbling a little. "Yeah. Him. Again, should've spoken up sooner when I saw things weren't right."

"But you turned out all right," I said. "What's the third?"

"What?"

"What's the third regret? You said you had three but you only told me two," I pointed out.

Grandma laughed. "Can't a person have any secrets around you?"

"No way! Spill."

Grandma shifted in her seat. "The last one isn't

something I didn't say. It's something I said. When Molly was born, I used the *r* word to tell you about her."

"It's okay, you didn't—"

"Let me finish, toots." Grandma squeezed the steering wheel so hard, I saw her knuckles pop out white. "I wish I hadn't been the one who introduced you to that word. I wish I hadn't even thought that word. When I see Molly now, and I think about how sad my thoughts were when that sweet girl was born—"

"It's okay, Grandma." I leaned forward and squeezed her shoulder. "You didn't know any better then. But now you do."

Grandma didn't say anything, just loosened her grip on the steering wheel and then patted my hand. "Well, no matter how things go with the election, I have an important role for you soon enough."

This time I arched an eyebrow, making Grandma chuckle. "Flower girl. At the wedding. It's only a few weeks away."

That again. I sat back and tucked my face under my T-shirt again.

❖ ❖ ❖

I smoothed my hair in the mirror of the girls' bathroom the next morning. To prepare, I had looked through as many pictures of presidents as possible. Just about all of them, from the first to current president, seemed to go for brushing all of their hair back with a little flair and then using enough gunk to keep it from moving or otherwise looking like human hair. I had combed back the sides of my hair, slicking them into place with hair gel I found under the sink in Mom and Dad's bathroom. My bangs sort of flopped down, so I filled my hands with water and plastered them back, too.

"How do I look?" I asked Amanda, who sat on the sink ledge next to me.

"Different," she said. I cocked an eyebrow at my friend. *Different* was an understatement to how *she* looked. Her hair was once again framing her face in soft layers. She wore a navy dress with red polka dots and high boots.

"Just how much clothing did you and Mom buy last week?"

Amanda grinned. "Dad gave me his credit card, and I had six years' worth of birthday money."

"Six years?" I paused in slicking my hair.

"Yeah, I hadn't seen anything I wanted."

"For *six years*?"

Amanda shrugged. "Fashion wasn't really on my radar." She twisted her neck, making the tendons pop with a sound I felt in my knees. "Fashion used to make me mad." Her face set. "Now I get mad thinking about all the dresses I could've worn."

The debates were right after the morning announcements. All morning long, Dad, who had driven me to school since I told him I needed extra time to get ready, asked me if I was sure about things. *Are you sure you want your hair to look like that? Are you sure that's the outfit you want to wear?* Looking at my slicked back hair and presidential reflection now, I nodded. "I'm sure," I said right out loud.

"Sure about what?" Amanda asked.

"Everything. And thanks for picking out this outfit for me." I smoothed the sides of my jacket, too.

"Your mom pushed for a dress, but I know you really wanted something presidential with some Lucy flair." Amanda chewed on the corner of her fingernail. "Hey, after all this election stuff is over, can you help me out with something?"

"Of course," I said. "You don't have to wait until after the elections. What do you need?"

Amanda stared down at her shoes. "No, nothing to

worry about now. Just maybe I could use some help on Saturday."

"Saturday?" I pinched my cheeks. Amanda's were glowy and pink and mine were just pasty and shiny.

"Yeah." Amanda crossed her arms and still didn't look up. "Days of Yonder Faire is this weekend."

"If your dad needs someone to walk the plank, you should know I'm not good with heights. I fall off the sidewalk all the time. Once I even broke a finger."

Amanda laughed, but it didn't sound right, not like her usual bursting-out-of-her laughs. "No, my dad's part of the Ye Olde Time Festival. Days of Yonder Faire has, um, my . . . um, mom."

"Your mom?"

"Yeah."

The door slammed open and Amanda's face shut down. "Whatever you need," I said quickly before whoever entered could hear us. "I'll help you."

"Thanks." Amanda rubbed at the corner of her eyes.

Whoever had entered the bathroom stomped down the short hall to where Amanda and I were stationed in front of the mirrors. I looked in the mirror to see Becky standing just behind me. If Grandma were here, she'd tell her to close her mouth before a fly landed on her tongue.

Becky gasped. Her hands flew to her cheeks. "What. Are. You. Wearing?" The last word pitched so high it echoed in my head.

I glanced down at my outfit. "Presidential stuff."

"I didn't mean a pantsuit! I didn't even know kids our age could find a pantsuit! Why is it red?" Becky's hands were in fists at her side. "And your hair!"

"You're doing a lot of yelling," I said. "It's not very vice presidential."

"Have you ever seen a president with a wet mullet? You look crazy."

I smoothed my hair again, shaking drips of water from my hands. "I think you're too obsessed with hair and clothes." I glanced at Amanda. "It's an epidemic."

"I think you're not nearly obsessed enough." Becky threw up her hands. Then she rubbed the heels of her hands into her eyes. Suddenly she looked like a raccoon. Was she wearing makeup?

"Am I the only one *not* wearing makeup?" I hate when I think out loud. Amanda paused in smearing on some lip gloss.

"Good idea," Becky said. She unzipped her backpack and pulled out a tiny purse. "Sit down and try not to blink."

❖ ❖ ❖

Miss Parker did blink at me a few times as I walked across the stage to my podium a few minutes later. Sam was on my left, Tom to the right. Miss Parker stood with a microphone to the side of the stage.

The mascara Becky had swiped around my eyes stuck a blurry black frame around everything I saw. And I no longer had to worry about blushing too much while speaking. The red circles she brushed onto my cheeks took care of that issue. I only wished my lips didn't smack together so much. Maybe the lip gloss was actually glue? Becky said it was important to put the makeup on thick so the folks in the back could see it, too. She called it "stage makeup." At least my hair was on point. I smoothed it again as I walked; yep, still slick.

Tom wore his usual get-up—track pants, sweatshirt, and snorty half grin. He snickered as I passed him. Whatever. Sam looked really nice. His curly hair was combed to the side. He had a shirt with buttons, and had even tucked it into his jeans. His brown eyes widened and he also blinked a bunch of times as I approached my podium. I tried to smile at him in a reassuring yet presidential way. Sam's eyebrows scrunched together as his eyes darted from my black eyelashes to my red cheeks to my shiny glue mouth, and then he looked away.

Quickly I wiped at my mouth and cheeks with my sleeves. When I glanced out in the crowd, Becky shook her head at me.

Most of the fifth grade still was trickling into the auditorium. I hadn't realized how many kids were in our grade. I gulped. Next to me, Sam shuffled some papers on his podium. Oh man! I hadn't printed out a speech at all! I was just going to talk. What if everyone thought I wasn't prepared enough? Tom, on my other side, nodded and grinned as his buddies came into the room. He didn't have notes, either.

Miss Parker interrupted my panic. She handed me a tissue and pointed to the sides of her mouth. Under her breath, she said, "You have a few smears." I dabbed at my face. She pointed to a few other spots. I swiped at those. She pointed to another spot on my chin. Finally she nodded and held out her hand for the tissue. It was orange and red and pink. Miss Parker plucked it from my hand with her fingertips. My first act as president was going to be banning makeup. "Just be yourself," Miss Parker whispered.

Earlier, Tom, Sam, and I had drawn numbers from a bucket to determine the order of who had to speak first. I picked number one, Tom was second, and Sam was last.

As everyone took a seat, the auditorium quieted and suddenly the only sound was *bam, bam, bam.* Then Miss Parker cleared her throat and the sound got louder and faster. *Bambambambambam.* Why wasn't anyone else freaking out about the booming?

"We're going to give each of our candidates five minutes to share their thoughts. The other candidates won't be able to interrupt during this time. Then we'll move on to the debate, during which each candidate will answer one question from the audience. At the end of the day, we vote!" *Bambambambambam.*

Miss Parker smiled over her shoulder at all of us, and once again the light glinted on her superhero teeth. She held up her phone, set to timer mode, and hit start. "Lucy will begin." *Bambambambambambam.* I sucked in a big breath and realized the banging was my stupid heart.

We can do this, I told myself. Only I forgot to say it silently. Next to me, Tom snorted and people in the audience laughed. I swallowed, scrunching shut my eyes for a second. Opening them took a second too long since the lashes got all tangled thanks to the mascara globs.

"Hi," I said. Again Tom snorted.

Miss Parker cut in, "Just a reminder. Each candidate only has five minutes to speak *and* no other candidate or audience member may interrupt the candidates as they speak." She smiled. "Go ahead, Lucy."

I nodded. "I am Lucy Beaner, and I'm running for class president because I know what it's like to not be listened to and I want to be the one who listens to you." I spotted Bree in the front row; she smiled back at me. "I have a lot of ideas."

"Yeah, stealing goats was a good one!" Henry shouted out from the crowd.

Miss Parker again said that no one should interrupt, but I felt my cheeks burn brighter than a whole pot of Becky's blush as everyone started laughing. Someone in the back neighed, even though that's something horses, not goats, do.

I huffed out of my nose. "I have a lot of good ideas," I said again. "Some of you heard me talking about clubs." I spotted Kyle in the crowd, sitting next to an empty seat. "I think we should have the chance to have clubs, like maybe a comic trading club, or musical theater club, or a Down with the Patriarchy club." The girl with the blue streak in her hair let out a *woot, woot.* I smiled and let out the air I hadn't realized I had locked up in my chest. "You know, any issue we care about, we could see if other people care about it, too, and then set up a time to meet.

I'd get teachers or parents to help out. Maybe we could even have clubs for the stuff that annoys teachers, so we wouldn't get in trouble for sneaking it in. We'd have a set time to do it instead. Stuff like Pokemon trading or Roblox. Stuff like that." A couple people nodded and I took a deep breath. *We're doing this.*

Just then someone else let out another neigh. Henry held up a poster with Tomkin the Goat on it.

Bambambambam. "Be a hero," I said, even though it didn't make any sense. I coughed and Tom snorted. "I mean, being a hero is important. Sam is a hero. Tom says he's a hero, and I guess that's debatable." A few people clapped, and I realized the claps were for my opponents. "I'm not a hero."

"You can say that again," Tom quipped into his microphone, ignoring Miss Parker's call to be quiet. The whole class laughed, going from soft little snickers to full-out guffaws.

Miss Parker held up her hand to signal silence.

When they did quiet, I did just what Tom suggested. I said it again. "I'm not a hero. I want to be. I admire heroes, people in history like George Washington, who wasn't afraid to do things in a different way, and Eleanor Roosevelt, who wasn't afraid to be unpopular if it meant she could be right, and Harriet Tubman, who didn't stop when she had what she needed but made sure her friends did, too. I want to be like that. I'm working on it." The room was so quiet then I could hear that bam of my heart filling the silence. "And I have another idea. Maybe we could bring in other heroes? People who do big things in our community, like the EMTs who helped save Sam after he saved those babies." More clapping, not for me. "People like doctors and firefighters and police officers. They could tell us how to be heroes, too. Maybe they could come in once a month and talk to us. We could have a box in the cafeteria, where we put the names of people we think are heroes.

"I'm not brave like them. But I could learn how to be."

Miss Parker met my eye and smiled. She held up two fingers. That's how many minutes I had left.

I nodded. In the front row, I saw Sheldon watching me. Even though he was on Sam's side he smiled. "And I have another idea. It's about the turtles."

In the audience, Henry started chanting, "Build the climbing wall! Build the climbing wall! Build the climbing wall!" Even though Tom wasn't chanting along, he shook his fist to the beat.

"Silence!" Miss Parker called. "Anyone disrupting will have to leave the auditorium."

"We can't stop the turtles from choosing our

playground as their hatching ground, but that doesn't mean we have to give up the playground, too." Next to me Sam said, "What?" at the same time Sheldon gasped in the audience.

Buzz! Miss Parker's timer went off.

"Let me finish!" I said. "I think we should create—"

"Time's up, Lucy," Miss Parker said.

"But I—"

Before I could finish, Tom leaned into the microphone and began his speech. I half turned toward Sam, sure he'd know that I hadn't been able to finish. That he'd know I cared about Sheldon and the turtles. Sam stared down at his notes. I glanced to Sheldon. He sat with his arms crossed and head down.

"If I could just finish my sent—"

"So rude!" Tom shook his head. People in the crowd booed and I knew it was at me, not him. "My turn to speak."

"You mean *lie*."

"Whatever, goat-napper."

"Enough!" Miss Parker shook her head. "Tom, go ahead."

I sighed and crossed my arms. *This ought to be good.*

If only I had known how much worse life was going to get.

Chapter Nineteen

"You know me as a winner," Tom said, smirking out at everyone. "And you're right. I get hat tricks every soccer game. I never let my team down. I'm a winner. And if you vote for me, you'll be a winner, too. We'll have the best fifth grade ever. We'll have our playground the way it was meant to be, complete with the climbing wall. Look, turtles have their houses on their backs. They'll be fine."

"They won't!" Sheldon shouted. "They won't be fine! Unless you think dead is fine."

Miss Parker shushed Sheldon but Tom just laughed. "Whatever. Look, I like all of you and you all like me. There's not much to think about here. You could vote for me." He pointed to himself with his thumbs and grinned.

"Or you could vote for that." He jabbed his thumb in my direction and a bunch of people laughed. "I mean, she was so upset about running against me that she stole my grandpa's goat." Tom shook his head as a few people in the crowd murmured.

"That's not true!" I yelped. "I didn't steal him!"

"Lucy!" Miss Parker said. "No interruptions. Let's keep to the issues, Tom."

"Right, Miss Parker." Tom smirked at me. "The issue is that I'm honest. I'm popular. I'm a winner. Vote for me and you'll be, too. Vote for me, and I'll race you up the best climbing wall you've ever seen, right here on our playground. Vote for me, your next president."

The crowd, led by Henry's chant of *Tom, Tom, Tom, Tom*, erupted into cheers. The timer still hadn't gone off. "Can I have his extra minute?" I asked over the noise.

"First she tries to steal a goat, then she tries to steal my time," Tom quipped.

"I did *not* steal the goat!" I yelled.

"Wrong."

"At least I'm not named after a goat, Tomkin," I hissed.

"Everyone settle down!" Miss Parker called. She had never yelled before that I could remember. Usually just raising her hand for quiet or a firm *stop it* got everyone to still. The yell to settle down seemed to echo around the room. Everyone stopped.

"Lucy, Tom, I remind you that we're to behave with dignity and integrity." She shook her head at us both. "Okay, one more candidate. I remind the audience, as well, that we need to be silent listeners and supporters of our candidates." She turned back to the podium. "Go ahead, Sam."

Tom snorted again. I rubbed at my mascara-clogged eyes to better see Sam. He stood there like a guppy, mouth opening and closing. I've seen this look a lot, but usually it's directed at me after I've said something he considers unusual, I guess ("What do you think life would be like if our feet were our hands and we walked on those hands?" or "Let's not use our thumbs today!"). It's his I-have-no-idea-what-to-say face.

Look at your notes! I stared hard at the papers on the podium, trying to will him to notice them again. *Come on, Sam. You can do this.* He didn't move.

Miss Parker stood in front of Sam, whispering quietly to him. He nodded and picked up the papers. Because of his cast, Sam could only hold the papers in one hand. That hand shook, making the papers rattle. Sam suddenly looked really pale, and the shining lights over him made the beads of sweat along his forehead sparkle. He blinked and rubbed at his eyes. For some reason, that made my own eyes tear up. *Come on, Sam!*

Tom snorted again as Sam cleared his throat. "Shut it, Tomkin," I snapped.

Miss Parker arched an eyebrow at me but quickly put her attention back to Sam. "Whenever you're ready, Sam."

Sam cleared his throat again. "I'm, um, Sam. And I'm, um, running for president?" He squished his eyes shut again and stared down at his notes. "My vice president, Sheldon, and I focus on the turtles? On protection?" Everything he said ended high-pitched like a question. In the audience, Henry laughed. A few more people joined in. Sam's mouth opened and closed a few more times. "We care about keeping them safe?"

I glanced down at Sheldon, whose eyes bulged out and whose mouth was silently moving with words I was sure he wanted Sam to recite.

"Okay," Miss Parker asked. "And how would you help the turtles?"

"We'd, um, partition off that part of the playground. Make it a turtle-safe zone?"

Miss Parker nodded. When Sam didn't say anything else, she prompted, "What else would you do as president?"

"Right," Sam said and looked again at the papers.

Clumsily, he tried to flip to the next page, even though the first was covered top to bottom in his careful handwriting and all he had said (asked, really) was that he'd help the turtles. "We'd talk with parents about issues and—"

"Parents?" Tom scoffed.

Sam looked up quickly at Tom, then his eyes snagged on the audience.

Once I had seen a poor spider spin around the swirling soapy water at the bottom of the shower before slipping down the drain after I accidentally-on-purpose splashed it from its web. Sam was acting a lot like that spider, spiraling down the drain.

"We care about making sure everybody feels . . . you know." Sam wiped at his forehead again. His cast hit the microphone, making a crackling noise pour across the auditorium.

"Everyone feels what, Sam?" Miss Parker asked.

"Feels, um, safe. Feels good about coming to school." Sam swallowed. "I'm, um. I'm not feeling good."

Sam's skin went from pale to green. His eyes suddenly looked huge. "I'm not—" His shoulders jerked back a little, then rolled suddenly forward.

"Oh, no!" Miss Parker's eyes widened but she didn't move.

Sam's mouth made a perfect circle. His shoulders jumped upward and he bent forward. His casted arm wrapped awkwardly around his middle and his other hand flew to his mouth. "Oh, no!" I blurted and the words seemed to hook Sam's attention. He whipped to the side, toward me. *Heroes act!* I couldn't let my best friend flail on his own. I rushed toward him. I'd catch him before he passed out.

"I'll catch you!" I cried. I jumped off my podium step toward Sam, arms out and mouth open to tell him again that I'd catch him.

For some reason, for just a second, time stopped. Everything slowed down. I was able to have complete, complicated thoughts in the space of a few seconds. I didn't know why, but my thought maker reflected back on the moment when we learned the names of the wolves in the Able Wolf Sanctuary. When April's aunt Shelley told us the new wolf was named Ralph, I'd said, "My dad says ralph instead of puke."

A rumbling, clogged-drain noise spilled from Sam's lips as he fell toward me.

And then he ralphed all over my pantsuited self.

❖ ❖ ❖

Everything stopped. No one spoke. The only sounds

were splats as bits of Sam's unchewed scrambled eggs and toast dripped from my arms onto the stage floor. Plop. Plop. Plop.

In front of me, Sam straightened. His eyes closed and his face went from pasty white to cherry red. He shook his head and his eyes opened again. I stood there, still with arms outstretched. Still ralphified. Water pooled in Sam's eyes.

And that's when the silence shattered. Some of the people in the audience, such as Lily, gasped and pressed their hands over their mouths. Shemanda jumped to their feet. Sheldon shouted, "It's okay, man!" Amanda turned toward Henry, who was laughing and pointing, and growled. She cracked her knuckles and seemed ready to lunge toward Henry if Sheldon hadn't grabbed her shoulder, turning her back toward Sam. "Kumbaya, Sam!" she called out.

But most of the people? They were acting like Henry, holding their stomachs and laughing way too loudly, or like Becky, who covered her mouth with her hand and made choking, puking sounds.

Miss Parker stretched her hand toward Sam. "It's okay, Sam." She glanced toward me. A glob of something fell off my still-outstretched arms. "Okay, Lucy?"

I nodded and slowly lowered my arms.

Miss Parker turned back to the audience. By then, several other teachers had been quieting their classes, too, so the noise was more of a hiss now. "We're going to do away with the debate section. Let's all head back to our classrooms."

I didn't see Sam after that. Miss Parker told me to head down to the locker room to shower and find a change of clothes in the Lost and Found. I spent the rest of the day wearing yet another Lost and Found outfit (too-tight brown corduroy pants and a purple turtleneck with pink bunnies all over it) and, though I had scrubbed at my hair with the thin pink soap in the shower dispensers, I caught a whiff of the rotting peach scent of the recently ralphed-upon whenever I shifted too fast in any direction. The mascara Becky had splotched onto my eyes wouldn't come off with the water or the burny soap, so I looked like a sleep-deprived panda. The nurse offered to call home and have Mom or Dad pick me up for the day, but I didn't want to miss the elections. I had to make my vote count.

That afternoon, just before we all filled out a ballot for fifth-grade class president, Ms. Drake interrupted classes through the loudspeaker so Sheldon could share a quick speech about his and Sam's platform. "Sam Righter, one of the presidential candidates, has gone home for the day." A few rows over from me, Tom snorted. I growled.

Sheldon talked about how the turtles are endangered, about how more animals are endangered every year and while we couldn't save all of them, we should save the ones we could. He talked about how extinction was forever.

Know what else is extinct?

Chances of winning the presidency if you've been publicly puked upon during the debate.

Know how I know?

Lily helped count the votes. I heard her whispering to someone in the bus line. Tom won, earning ninety-six votes. Sam, despite never giving his speech and being said puker, received six votes. And me?

"Only two votes," Lily had whispered. "That's it." Both of their mouths dropped when I accidentally-on-purpose bumped against them on the way to my bus.

Two.

Two votes in the entire class. Even worse, that meant almost half the class didn't even bother voting.

I slicked my hair for two votes. For just about nothing. I had scouted out my school's problems and figured out how to solve them for nothing. I had put myself out there for nothing. I had been laughed at, made fun of, and talked about for nothing. Nothing.

Worst of all, I had lost my best friend for nothing.

Chapter Twenty

Grandma's station wagon was in the driveway when I got home after school. Mom and Dad wouldn't be home until close to five o'clock since Molly had an optometrist appointment. Grandma sat on the front porch, slowly rocking in one of the wicker chairs. Her arms were crossed. "How'd it go, toots?"

"How'd what go?" I walked by her and yanked open the door. Grandma trailed behind me as I dumped my backpack by the door.

I was going to grab some chocolate in the kitchen but Mr. Bosserman was there by the coffee pot. He pulled two mugs out of the cabinet like this was his house. "Lucy," he said with a nod. His dark eyes took in the black smudges on my face and then dropped down to my lost-and-found outfit.

"I thought your mom and Amanda picked out a new outfit for the day?" Grandma asked. Awesome. Now she and Mr. Bosserman were finishing each other's thoughts.

I lifted up the plastic bag filled with my puked-upon pantsuit and crumbled dreams. Grandma winced. Probably a whiff of the stinky clothes had drifted out from the bag when I shook it. I didn't smell it anymore. I was immune to horrible scents and experiences, I guessed.

"How was the election?" Mr. Bosserman asked.

Grandma sat in the kitchen chair across from where I stood. She grabbed my wrist gently.

"I lost." I yanked my arm from her grip. "Surprised?" This time I was the one to cock an eyebrow. Grandma's face flushed for a moment and her face sort of smooshed, but it wasn't with surprise.

"Well, you figured it was a bit of a long shot, didn't you?" Grandma tried to put her arm around me, but I dodged her on the way to the bathroom. I crammed my pantsuit bag into the trash can by the toilet and showered until all I smelled was soap.

When I came back down the hall wearing sweatpants and a fluffy sweatshirt, I thought Grandma and Mr. Bosserman would have left.

But both were just where I had left them, in the

kitchen. I peeked around the corner. They sat at the kitchen table with their backs to me, drinking coffee and talking quietly. Mr. Bosserman was telling Grandma about the geysers in Yellowstone. "The ground around them is bright as a rainbow—yellows, pinks, blues. You feel like you're visiting Mars, and then out of nowhere, a bison struts right up and plops himself down on the edge of it."

"Sounds amazing." Grandma slurped coffee.

"What's really amazing are the stars," Mr. Bosserman said. "I know they're the same ones we got here, onest. But they're bigger. Brighter. Better. Can't wait to show you 'em."

Grandma slid her hand into Mr. Bosserman's where it rested next to his mug. "Can't wait to see them with you." Her faced turned toward his, and I saw her cheeks rise in a wide smile. "But won't you be bored, seeing all of these places you've already been?"

Mr. Bosserman's voice dipped. I leaned into the entranceway a bit more to hear him, reaching out to steady a rack of baskets I had knocked into before they could rustle. "You haven't seen them," he said, "so I'll get to see them all over again for the first time right along with you."

I almost slunk back down the hall to my room after that, but then I heard my name. I didn't catch the rest of what Grandma said, only my name.

"Ah, she'll be all right," Mr. Bosserman said. "Kid's got grit, just like someone else I know."

I dropped down to all fours and crawled to the entranceway. Grandma and Mr. Bosserman still were holding hands. Grandma sighed. "She never chooses the easy way, you know?"

Mr. Bosserman chuckled. "Like I said, onest. She gets it honest."

"I'm going to miss a lot, going with you."

Mr. Bosserman nodded. "You will."

"But I'll see stars. And geysers. And you."

"And those girls of ours will see it's never too late to take on the world."

When their faces tilted toward each other, I ducked down the hall for real. A few minutes later, Grandma knocked on my bedroom door. When I opened it, there was a bowl of Nutella and chocolate popcorn waiting for me with a note. *We're ready to watch a movie when you're ready to join us.*

❖ ❖ ❖

When Mom and Dad came home a couple hours later, Mr. Bosserman was snoring on the couch and the credits were rolling on Grandma's and my favorite movie. It's about an alien that lands in the woods and a boy who helps it call home. It was made way back in the eighties, and, based on the clothing, I was pretty sure that the lost-and-found outfit I had been wearing most of the day was brand new when the movie had been released. Grandma said it was the first movie she had ever taken Mom to see in the theater.

I tried picturing Mom my age and couldn't do it. "Do I remind you of Mom when she was my age?"

Grandma ran her finger along the popcorn bowl to get a smudge of Nutella. "You have her big brown eyes."

I elbowed her a little so she'd really answer the question.

"Your mom, though, was quiet. Never caused any trouble."

I crossed my arms. Did I cause trouble? I sighed.

Grandma nudged me back. "Sometimes people need to cause trouble. Especially if they're doing it to fix problems."

Dad threw open the door before I could think through what Grandma had said. "May I present," he said in a dramatic voice, "the new and improved, bespectacled Molly Irene Beaner!"

And then Mom jumped through the door holding Molly facing outward toward us. Molly wore black-framed glasses, as round as Harry Potter's, and held in place with a strap around her head. She was wearing a white lacy turtleneck with a black sweater and pants, so she totally looked like a little businesswoman. Molly waved her arms and kicked her legs, smiling so wide a line of drool seeped out. "Doesn't she look like a mini Ruth Bader Ginsburg?" Mom laughed. "Minus the drool."

"She does!" I jumped up and clapped, making Molly giggle.

"I'm surprised you know who that is," Mom said.

"Oh, yeah, Miss Parker has taught us all about super-heroes and leaders. I know all of the Supreme Court justices."

"Impressive." Mom handed Molly to me. Mom and Dad had told me before the appointment that because of her Down syndrome, Molly was much more likely to have problems with her eyes, and so I wasn't surprised to see her with glasses. But I was surprised at how completely adorable they were on my sister. She batted at the glasses a little and Mom reached over me to lower Molly's hands.

Molly leaned forward and hit me with a slobbery kiss on the cheek. I looked forward to the day when she remembered to close her mouth before kissing me. When I glanced up, I noticed Mom, Dad, and Grandma exchanging glances. All three of them looked away.

"So, yeah, I didn't win. But I did get two votes." I gave Molly a high five. "Go me."

Dad closed the door as quietly as he had burst through it a few moments earlier. "I'm sorry, kiddo."

I shrugged. Molly giggled at the little bounce. "It was a long shot, right?"

"Do you want to talk about it?" Mom asked. She smoothed the side of my hair. Her brow wrinkled a little. I knew she was surprised at the still-damp locks. I didn't usually voluntarily shower.

I nodded. "But not right now, okay?"

"Okay," Dad said.

I carried Molly over to where we always keep a blanket spread out and lowered her onto it, settling beside her. Molly whimpered a little and batted at the glasses. I lowered her hands and blew raspberries on her belly to distract her. She twisted to roll onto her stomach and bunched her fists. Three seconds until epic werebaby screech. . . .

Right on cue, Molly erupted. Mom swooped her back up into her arms. "How about a nice diaper change?" Molly didn't seem too excited by the idea, to be honest.

A second or two after they headed back toward Molly's room, Grandma pushed herself up off the couch and followed Mom down the hall. I figured she and Dad must've exchanged another conversation look since Dad sank down on the blanket beside me.

"I don't want to talk about it yet," I said. "But there's a puke-covered pantsuit in the bathroom. That's all you need to know."

Dad rubbed at his chin. "You tossed your cookies, huh?"

"What?"

"Had a visit from Barfello Bill?"

"Are you—"

"Decided to leggo your Eggo?"

"Stop."

"Launched your lunch?"

I sighed. If you can't beat them, join them. "Sam cashed in his round-trip meal ticket," I said, knowing it was Dad's favorite vomitism. (Since Molly, he's had a lot of opportunity to work on his puking-related vocab.) "All over me."

"Ew." Dad shuddered.

"On stage," I added.

"Oh, my."

"Before the debate."

"I see." This time, Dad sighed.

For a moment, neither of us said anything. Then Dad put his arm around me. "Sounds like a terrible day."

I rested my head against his shoulder. "I really thought I could win," I blurted.

Dad squeezed me. "I did, too." He pulled in a big breath. "You would've been a great president, Lucy, and I'm so incredibly proud of you for trying."

"Well," I said, "I guess that's that. Still on the search for my awesome."

"Not so fast." Dad squeezed me again. "Just because you didn't win the election doesn't mean you don't have good ideas. I heard you prepping your speech. Your plans are solid. They're awesome."

"So what?" I said. "I lost."

Dad shook his head. "You lost the first battle. If you really care about and believe in your ideas, you've got to pick yourself up. Keep going."

"How am I supposed to do that? I'm out of pantsuits."

"There's a school board meeting next week. Every meeting, there are opportunities for the public to speak. Tell them your ideas, especially the one about the turtles. See what you can do." Dad patted the side of my head. "And your other ideas—the ones about clubs and heroes—you *could* work with your new president and with the principal on those."

This time, I was the one to shudder. Work with Tomkin the Human? I'd *almost* rather be hit with another Sam splash. But I could talk with Ms. Drake. And maybe I could write down the ideas and share them with Tom. A mean thought wormed its way into my problem-solving thought maker. If I did those things, jerkface Tomkin the Human would get the credit for implementing them. "I really wanted to be a hero," I mumbled. "I wanted to be the one making the difference. I wanted it to be the thing that made me awesome."

"Well," Dad said. "You've got a decision to make. What's more important to you—making a difference or getting the credit? Sometimes, you can even get *more* done when you aren't the one officially in charge because you can focus on each issue. Poor Tom, he's got to listen to everyone's issues now. Including yours." Dad smiled. "You can still be a leader without being *the* leader." He nudged me. "Having grit, shaking yourself off, and standing back up when you fall down? Not everyone has that. Not everyone is awesome enough to have that."

"Can I use the laptop?" I popped up to my feet. "I have some research to do and emails to send."

"That's my girl."

Chapter Twenty-one

The next day, I went to school expecting to be made fun of. And yeah, lots of people did make puking sounds when they passed me. Some people still talked about goat-napping. And Tomkin the Human was more braggy than I thought possible, thanking everyone for voting for him and talking nonstop about how he won.

But a lot of people smiled at me, too. Some said hi in the hallway. And it wasn't *that* bad. Except that Sam didn't come back to school until Thursday, and then he still ate his lunches in the library even though he didn't have the making-posters excuse any more. Sheldon said he'd be back when he was ready and we needed to give Sam space.

Saturday morning, I woke up to the sound of the

doorbell. So did Molly. I rolled over to my side and covered my ears with my pillow. A few seconds later, Mom called my name over Molly's outraged cries.

I stumbled down the hall in my nightgown and rubbed at my eyes. Who would be coming over first thing on a Saturday morning like this? My thought maker bloomed a little heart-pounding *maybe. Maybe it's Ms. Drake. Maybe there was a massive miscount. Maybe I was president after all. Or maybe there was a long-forgotten presidential election rule that if you were ralphed upon, you immediately won a million sympathy votes.* I paused to straighten my hair and smooth my nightgown. I had to look surprised at my turn of fortunes but still composed. Presidential.

But when I entered the living room, Amanda, not Ms. Drake, stood there. "Hey," she said. "Ready?"

I glanced down at my nightgown. "For what?"

"Days of Yonder Faire!" Amanda crossed her arms. Her face fell into a scowl. "You forgot, didn't you?"

"No!" I blurted, even though, yeah, I had. "You never said you were picking me up. Or what time or anything."

"I'm not picking you up," Amanda said. "I walked here."

Mom stepped forward, peeking out the window for Mr. Frankston's car. "But that's three miles, at least. You must've walked in the dark. Does your dad know where you are?"

Amanda shrugged. "I told him I'd be with you guys today."

"But why didn't you call us?" Mom asked. "We would've picked you up."

"He had to be at Ye Olde Time Festival pretty early."

Mom blinked. "But you want to go to Days of Yonder Faire? Isn't that near Litchfield, about an hour from here?"

Amanda's cheeks turned pink, and it wasn't from makeup. Her mom was going to be at the Faire. I guessed I'd act a little strange, too, if I were about to see my mom for the first time in about ten years.

"Amanda spends so much time at her dad's festivals. Can you take us to the Faire?" I asked.

Mom chewed her lip. I knew her mom sensor was bleeping, detecting that something she didn't understand was happening.

"Please?" I bounced. "You could dress up Molly in that little princess dress. Maybe get her one of those pointy hats!"

"Sheldon's going to be there, too," Amanda said. "He's putting up a Save the Shelled Ones table."

Dad, who had been leaning against the doorway,

cleared his throat. "Sounds like Sheldon's not ready to give in, either."

I smiled. Poor Tomkin the Human. He didn't know what he was in for, now that both Sheldon and I would be after him. Maybe now that Sheldon and I weren't running against each other, he'd hear out my idea for the turtles. Maybe we could join forces. I turned my grin on Dad. "How about it, Daddy-o? Can we go to the Faire?"

Dad crossed his arms. "Amanda, can you verify that there will be giant turkey legs?"

Amanda nodded solemnly. "My dad says all Faires and festivals are contractually obligated to have turkey legs if they mention days long past."

"Excellent." Dad tilted his head toward Mom.

"You had me at pointy princess hats." She yawned. "First coffee, then breakfast, then Faire."

"I can make some eggs while you guys get ready," Amanda offered. She pushed up her sleeves and strode toward the kitchen.

"No!" I yelped, remembering the puked-up scrambled eggs I recently wore on my pantsuit. I jumped in front of her and steered her toward the couch. "Let's just have toast."

"I hate toast," Amanda said.

"Okay, just plain bread, straight from the cupboard."

❖ ❖ ❖

As soon as Dad parked the car (and grumbled about the five-dollar parking fee), Amanda grabbed my hand. Her face was set like a statue.

"Everything okay?" Mom asked as she pulled Molly's stroller from the trunk and smeared sunscreen over her face.

Amanda nodded her head. She leaned in and whispered, "I checked the Faire website to make sure my mom's still the fortune-teller. She is. As soon as we step foot in there, she's going to know."

"Isn't that going to make things a ton easier?" I whispered back.

Amanda didn't move.

"Listen, we're here. We've got to go in." I opened my car door. Amanda lurched forward, grabbed the handle, and slammed it shut.

"Girls?" Dad asked.

"Just a sec," I replied.

I took a deep breath and put a hand on each side of Amanda's flaming face. "It's going to be okay. I promise.

But nothing will happen if you don't take action, and the whole reason we're here is that you're tired of nothing happening."

Amanda nodded, or maybe I made her nod with my hands. Either way, she sort of loosened like a wet noodle and soon we were on our way into the Days of Yonder Faire.

Dad consulted a map, looking for the best turkey leg joint. Suddenly he stopped, his arm outstretched like when he brakes too fast in the car and has to keep Molly's diaper bag from flying forward. "Is that a . . ."

"That's a papier-mâché turtle head," I clarified. Amanda rushed past me to Sheldon's Save the Shelled Ones table. I would've zoomed there, too, finally able to tell Sheldon my idea to save the turtles, except I saw who was sitting with him behind the table. Sam.

I stopped mid-step. "Sam," I said, but low as a whisper despite the huge swarms of people around us and the yards between us. He heard me anyway. Know how I know? Because he stood up from the table and stormed away in the opposite direction.

Sam walked with his arm cradled against his side. I wondered if it hurt. I wondered if he'd ever talk to me again. After Tom and Henry humiliated him in fourth grade, Sam didn't talk to me for a week. Not because he blamed me or anything, just because he was embarrassed.

"Was that Sam?" Mom asked.

I nodded.

"Have you spoken since . . . the incident?" Mom was much more restrained in her vomitisms.

I shook my head.

Mom curled in her bottom lip and stared at Sam's retreating body. "I think it's one of those things that will just take time. Speaking of which"—her eyes slid toward Dad—"I don't know how much longer we're going to be able to keep your father from his turkey leg."

"It's not even nine o'clock in the morning!"

"Turkey legs are a timeless treat," Dad called out. "They can't be constrained to afternoon alone." He sidestepped closer to Mom. "If we play our cards right, we can split one for breakfast and another for lunch."

Mom sighed. "I'm not sharing a turkey leg with you."

"You want your own, don't you?"

"Darn right." Mom handed me twenty dollars. "Here's a little spending cash. When you're ready for lunch, check in with me and Dad, okay?" She handed me sunscreen and waited until I smeared some on my face and arms. "Do you think Amanda has spending money?"

"Yeah, her dad always sends cash with her wherever she goes so she can avoid being hornswoggled."

"Hornswoggled? I assume that's pirate speak."

"Arr!" I swung my fist.

"So just text once every half hour so we know you're all right," Mom said to me. "If I text you and you don't reply in five minutes, I'm going to have them call your name over the loudspeaker and send the Faire sheriff after you. Got it?"

"Got it," I said and slipped my phone into my back pocket.

At the Save the Shelled Ones stand, Sheldon held out his hand to shake mine. "We held a nice campaign."

"Can we talk?" I asked after he shook. "I have an idea for the turtles, one that I think could make everyone happy."

"Lucy to the rescue once again." I twisted around to see Sam just behind me, lounging on the side of the Shelled Ones table. He scowled at me.

"What's that supposed to mean?" I snapped.

"I mean you're always butting in where you're not needed." Sam's mouth twisted. Every word he said felt like a pebble pelting me.

"I didn't make you throw up on stage," I yelled. "You did that on your own!"

"Yeah, and I would've been able to *leave* the stage if you hadn't planted yourself in my way. Thanks to you, I spewed in front of everyone!"

I shook my head. "Is that your way of saying sorry for throwing up all over me? I was trying to help you!"

"Why? Why can't you just leave me alone?"

I stomped my foot. "Because you're my friend. Friends help each other. Maybe you don't know that since you didn't have any friends before me, but that's what we do. We help each other!"

"Great, help me out then," Sam barked. "Leave me alone. That would be very helpful."

"Fine," I spit out.

"Fine," he said back.

We glared at each other for about an hour or maybe it was just a couple seconds. Sheldon cleared his throat. "So, Lucy, about that idea . . ."

I meant to answer, but a growl came out instead.

Amanda put her hand around my elbow. I hadn't realized I was shaking until I felt how steady her grip was against my skin. "Let's go for a walk."

"Fine," I said again, softer this time. Sam slouched down into a chair behind the Shelled Ones table.

We crunched through fallen leaves as we walked past

colorful tents filled with handcrafted hats and costumes, metal swords and wooden shields, and all sorts of baked and smoked foods. The air was a mixture of incense and sugar. A parade of medieval knights and princesses strolled by, waving and wishing us "good day." It should've been fun. Amanda and I should've been laughing and touching everything for sale. That twenty dollars should've been calling out to me to spend it. But neither of us spoke and neither of us smiled and neither of us spared one thought for the magic all around us.

"Do I meddle?" I asked.

Amanda didn't hesitate. "Yes."

I stopped walking.

"Well," Amanda said, "it's sort of your thing. That's why we're all friends, isn't it? Because you saw we were lonely or left out and you made a space for us at your table. You *and* Sam did that, actually." She sighed. "I'm glad you meddle. That's why I asked you to be here today. If you didn't meddle, April would still be picking her nose, Sam would still be a loner, I'd still be angry, and Sheldon . . . well, Sheldon would be exactly the same."

"I prefer to think of it as *helping*, not meddling," I grumped.

"Whatever. All I'm saying is it's not *always* a bad

thing. Sometimes it is—like when you set the eggs on fire and that time you lied about who liked each other. But most of the time it's helpful, really. I mean, that's why I asked you to help me today." She grinned. "I knew if I wanted to back out on meeting my mom, you wouldn't let me."

I smiled. "You're pretty smart, Amanda."

"Ah, since I stopped scaring everyone, I've been able to notice a lot more about them."

"Maybe you could help me figure out why Sam's such a jerk to me, then."

"Sam's angry," Amanda said like it was the most obvious thing in the world. I guess it was. "He's angry about his gymnastics days being over, about feeling weird when people suddenly like him, about upchucking on you in front of everyone. He's angry, and he's not used to being angry." Amanda shrugged. "I get it. I've been angry a long time. Angry is easy. There's always something to be angry about. Happy is harder. Happy is, like, a choice. It's a—"

"Decision," I cut in, thinking about when Mom and Dad decided to stop being sad that Molly had Down syndrome and start being happy about it instead. That's what they had called it—a decision to be happy. I pulled my phone from my pocket and punched out an *I'm fine* text to Mom and Dad before I forgot. "How can we make Sam decide to be happy?"

Amanda laughed. "We can't. My dad was always trying to make me stop being angry. Finally he just let me be angry, and that's when I wanted to stop."

"But he's blaming me for everything!" I stomped my foot again. "I mean, first he wants me to do stuff—like quit the election—because of him, then he wants me to totally leave him alone. I don't know why I'm the one he's always mad at!"

"Yeah, it's not right." Amanda twisted her neck, making all the bones pop and my knees hollow out. "Truth is, it makes me mad to see it. He doesn't get to be a jerk just because something bad happened to him. Bad things happen to everybody."

"So what do I do?" I asked.

Amanda shrugged. "You could stop being his friend."

"I don't want to do that," I whispered.

"So then you wait. But do me a favor, okay?" Amanda crossed her arms. "Don't let him keep being a jerk to you. Keep standing up to him. If you don't, then I'm going to have to beat him up, and I promised Sheldon I'd stop beating up people."

Suddenly Amanda's mouth dropped open and her eyes bulged.

"Is this your beating-up-people face?" I asked, then jumped about a mile into the air when someone's hands dropped onto my shoulders.

An eerie, wispy voice said, "I sense thoughts of violence and pain."

I whipped around and stared into the most peaceful, serene face I had ever seen. She wore about six different brightly colored scarves, all tied or draped around her narrow body. Her big green eyes blinked solemnly and her mouth fell in a soft smile. Her long wavy blonde hair fell below her waist and she wore more rings on her fingers than even Grandma. She blinked at us and squinted a little at Amanda, but I couldn't tell if there was any recognition. Then again, Amanda face was bulgy-eyed.

"I am Flora, the teller of fortunes," the lady said and bowed. "Care to enter my tent so I can share the future?" Flora's hand waved through the air as she said "future." She held open the tent flap and smiled at us both. Then she ducked into the tent, as if she just knew we'd follow right behind her.

I leaned into Amanda, who stood statue-still with her mouth hanging open and her eyes still huge. "This is her, right? Your mom?" I whispered.

Amanda nodded. "Dad gave me a picture. She looks older, but that's definitely her."

I stepped behind Amanda and did some meddling—I pushed her toward the tent. "Let's go!"

"She's going to know who I am," Amanda hissed.

"It didn't look like she knew who you were," I said. "Does she stay in touch with your dad? Or know that you guys live here?"

Amanda shook her head. "I don't think so."

"Then how would she know you? She hasn't seen you since you were a baby."

Amanda pointed to the sign hanging outside the tent. It was printed with PSYCHIC READINGS: I KNOW ALL ABOUT YOU ALREADY. The super confident, great-advice-giving girl I had seen a moment earlier was gone. This was a new Amanda. A scared Amanda. "What if—"

"Just go in!" I snapped. "What's the worst thing that could happen?"

Do me another favor, okay? Slap my face if I ever say that again. Just go ahead and slap it. Because the worst thing that could happen is always worse than you think it'll be.

Chapter Twenty-two

The inside of Flora the Fortune-Teller's tent was filled with clouds of misty incense. Framed mirrors hung from the tent poles. A stack of long yellowed cards and a crystal ball—a real crystal ball!—were on top of a table draped in red velvet.

"Fortune telling is an ancient art spanning through generations upon generations," Flora said in her whispery voice as she settled behind the velvet-draped table. "I will share the wisdom of my ancestors as I peek through the veil to see what lies ahead, warn of places where danger may await, and touch upon opportunities that might avail themselves in the days or years ahead. First, I will read your palms and then, perhaps, the mist will commune through the crystal ball." At these last words, the tent filled with music. I think it was flutes or pipes or angels, something like that.

"Did the crystal ball make the music?" I gasped.

Amanda crossed her arms. "She pressed a button in her pocket." I glanced at my friend. Her face was just angry lines. Uh-oh. Looked like Amanda had decided not to be happy.

"I see you are a skeptic," Flora said. "I will prove you wrong." She cleared her throat and pointed to metal bowl to the side of the crystal ball. In a much deeper voice she said, "Ten bucks a pop. Money in the bowl."

"Oh," I said. "Do you have change for a twenty?"

Resuming her mystical tone, Flora said, "I see two girls before me, both of whom," she suddenly gasped, her fingers floating to her mouth and her eyes darting around the shadowy room, before continuing in a even creepier voice, "have need of direction! Urgent direction!" She cleared her throat again and pointed to the bowl. A little sign in front was printed with TEN DOLLARS PER PERSON. YES, IF YOU'RE JUST LISTENING, YOU'RE A PERSON. PAY UP. Wow, she really had read my mind!

I dropped the twenty into the bowl.

"Who's first?" Flora held out both of her hands, palms up, when we sat on the two chairs in front of her table.

"Ama—" I started, but then Amanda elbowed me hard in the ribs.

"Don't tell her names. A fortune-teller should know," Amanda hissed.

Flora rubbed her temples. "I'm sensing something . . . *Amelia*."

Amanda snorted.

"Or perhaps," Flora squinted into the shadows, her lips moving silently, "it is *Amber*?"

Amanda held out her palm. "Amanda. My name's Amanda." I leaned forward, searching Flora's face. This was going to be it, I was sure of it. This would be the moment she knew her daughter was sitting in front of her.

But Flora just looked irritated as she reached over and grabbed Amanda's hand. "Sometimes the spirits jest." She stared at Amanda's hand, her fingers trailing along the different lines. "I see a long future in front of you."

"Well, I am eleven." Amanda rolled her eyes. "Not exactly psychic material."

"Knock it off," I whispered. I mouthed, *Decide to be happy*. Amanda rolled her eyes again.

Flora tilted her face from side to side. "I see a life filled with anger! I see sadness and betrayal! I see unbearable grief!"

I slowly slid my hands under my thighs. Who wanted to know stuff like that?

To my surprise, Amanda laughed. "I thought you saw the future, not the past."

Flora dropped Amanda's hand. "Look, kid," she said in a voice that was so much like Amanda's deep, gruff tone that I gasped. "What's your problem?"

"My problem?" Amanda jumped to her feet. "You're the fortune-teller!" She stormed out of the tent, ripping down one of the decorative scarves in her rush from the room. The sudden sunlight hurt my eyes.

Flora crossed her arms. "No refunds."

"What?"

"I said, no refunds. I don't care if your friend stormed out. That's not my problem." I totally had *not* been about to ask for change. Okay, so maybe I had been. But I wasn't really going to do it.

Flora tilted her head at me.

"You're a terrible fortune-teller!" I fumed.

Flora shrugged. "Can't win over everyone."

"And you're a turtle of a mom!"

"What?" Flora asked, but I stomped away without answering. "Wait!" she called. I turned back, expecting Flora to have finally figured out that Amanda was her daughter. Instead, she said, "Beware the green-headed monster!"

Whatever that means.

❖ ❖ ❖

I ran back toward the Shelled Ones table, figuring that would be where Amanda had taken off toward. I knew I was right when I passed knocked over trash cans and a ripped-in-half map. I sprinted faster.

Amanda stood in front of the Shelled Ones table. A note was taped to the table. *Went for funnel cake. Be back soon—Save the Shelled Ones, Sheldon*

I stood as close as I dared to Amanda, whose hands curled and uncurled into fists and whose breath came out in huffs through her nose.

"She didn't even know who I was!" Amanda whispered. "I thought she had to be thinking about me all of the time. I thought as soon as she saw me, she'd know. I thought she *thought* about me." Now her fists raised and slammed back down into her thighs.

"It's okay," I whispered. "We could talk to her—"

"No!" she growled. And then this sound, this horrible, ripping, aching scream just exploded out of Amanda.

"*No, no, no, no, no!*" And Amanda lurched forward. She grabbed the edge of the Shelled Ones table and whipped it over, sending T-shirts, pamphlets, and Sheldon's photographs of the turtles flying. Then Amanda jumped up and down, fists still slamming against her sides, on top of the wreckage. All the while, she screamed. "No, no, no, no! This isn't how it was supposed to go! She was supposed to miss *me*, too! She's supposed to *love* me, too!"

"I'm so sorry, Amanda." I reached toward her, but she whirled around, still stomping and crying. I was crying, too, I realized as one of the drips fell from my cheek and onto the ground. "But I don't think destroying Sheldon's stuff is going to make it better."

Amanda hiccupped. "Sheldon!" And then she was sobbing all over again. "Sheldon's going to be so mad at me!"

"We'll clean it up," I said, even though, of course there wasn't a chance.

I glanced around. Not only was the display destroyed, but a crowd now gathered around us, people whispering and pointing. Amanda covered her face in her hands. Sam pushed through the crowd. "What happened?" he gasped.

"Amanda," I whispered. "Her mom is here and didn't even recognize her. She sort of . . ." I pointed around at the destruction.

"Went Hulk?" Sam finished.

I nodded.

Beside us, Amanda hiccupped again. "He's going to be so mad!"

Just then the crowd parted for Sheldon, holding his giant papier-mâché head under his arm with a plate of funnel cake resting on top of it and his cheeks chipmunk full of cake. Amanda whimpered.

"I'm sorry," I blurted. I bit my lip when I saw Mom and Dad in the distance pushing Molly's stroller. Molly had on a pointy princess hat and Dad was gnawing on his turkey leg. I turned away from them and back to Sheldon. "It was my fault. I . . . I destroyed everything."

"Why?" Sheldon's face crumpled. "Why would you do this?"

"I, um. I was jealous of the attention you've been getting for Save the Shelled Ones." I hung my head, realizing that a big part of me wasn't lying at all. I was jealous.

Sam shook his head next to me but didn't say anything.

"Lucy, how could you?" Sheldon didn't even notice his funnel cake slide off the top of his giant turtle head.

Just then another voice, mystical and whispery,

floated out over us. "I sense this isn't the case." Flora the Fortune-Teller stood at the edge of the crowd. Great. Now she was psychic.

"It was me," a quiet voice that felt like a shout said. Amanda covered her face in her hands. "It was me, Sheldon. I'm so sorry. I was so upset and I came to talk to you and you weren't here, and I knew you wouldn't understand even if you had been." Amanda's shoulders shook as she cried.

Sheldon rushed toward her, throwing down his giant turtle head as he moved. It landed—*plop*—right on my foot.

"Yow!"

"Told you," Flora whispered and then disappeared back in the crowd.

"Hey!" I called after her. "You can't just leave."

But Flora was gone.

Sheldon patted Amanda's back. "What happened?"

"I saw my mom here," Amanda whispered. "And she didn't know it was me."

"Your mom? She's here?" Sheldon leaned against Amanda's side. "Why wouldn't you tell me?"

"She left me," Amanda whispered. "A long time ago. When I was just a baby. But I still thought . . ."

Sheldon put his arm around Amanda. Slowly the

people around us trickled away but Sam and I stayed put just behind them.

"It's okay," Amanda said. "I came. I saw. I freaked. I'm good. I don't need my mom."

I put my hand on Amanda's arm. "I'll share my mom."

Amanda nodded but didn't look up.

"You're going to be okay." Sheldon's voice was gentle. "Do you know why I love dinosaurs so much?"

"Because they're huge and powerful killing machines?" Amanda answered.

"Well, partly." Sheldon nodded. "But mostly it's because of my dad. He died when I was little. Mom told me he used to play with toy dinosaurs with me, making them roar. We'd go for walks, too, and look for dino tracks."

Amanda lowered her hands. "You never talk about your dad."

"You never talk about your mom."

"We should talk more," Amanda said.

"Yeah," Sheldon said. "We should. Maybe we can talk while we clean up this mess."

Amanda nodded and then righted the table she had knocked over. I bent to gather up some crumpled pamphlets but Sheldon stopped me. "We've got this." He glanced behind me at Sam.

"Lucy?" Sam said. He stared down at his sneakers. "Can we, maybe, go for a walk or something?"

We walked around the whole Faire three times but neither of us said a word. We weren't okay, but we weren't not okay, either.

Even worse: Flora the Fortune-Teller's tent was down by our third lap. She had run again.

Chapter Twenty-three

Miss Parker stood in front of the class about a month later. She smiled her superhero smile, teeth glinting. "Go ahead, Lucy," she said. "Share your superlatives."

I turned to the poster behind me and pointed to a picture I had drawn of my pack. "My favorite place is anywhere I can be with my friends."

"Yeah, all three of them." I bet you can guess who said that. If you didn't, you could've looked up on the board, where Miss Parker was writing Tom's name in marker.

"Four," I corrected. I pointed to the stick figures Amanda, Sheldon, Sam, and April, counting as I went. Tom's ears turned red but he didn't say anything else.

I moved to the part labeled *my bravest moment*.

"This is still blank because I don't think I've done it yet. I did *some* brave things, though. I'm going to do another soon. If you want to go to the PTO meeting on Thursday night, you'll see what I mean."

Tom snorted, and I heard the squeak of Miss Parker's marker as she circled his name on the board.

I moved to the hero emblem drawing. It was a wolf that still mostly looked like a spiky-legged llama, and it was wearing a cape. "This is my superhero emblem." I shrugged. "I like wolves."

"I do, too, Lucy," Lily whispered. I smiled at her. She called me Lucy instead of Lisa!

"Why's it have an *SD* on the cape?" someone asked.

"Oh." I grinned even wider. "That's for Super Dork. That's me. I'm a dork. So if I were a superhero, I guess I'd be a Super Dork."

I laughed, and soon everyone else did, too. It wasn't mean laughter, either.

The next drawing was me on the stage in a red pant-suit. "This is what I'm best known for. Getting puked on while on stage. Maybe you remember it." This time Miss Parker laughed harder than anyone.

❖ ❖ ❖

Thursday night, I once again wore a pantsuit.

Okay, so maybe it wasn't actually a pantsuit so much as it was a pair of black pants with a black sweater, but it made me feel like I was wearing a pantsuit. I didn't slick back my hair, though. And this time, it wouldn't end with me being covered in vomit.

I stood in front of the PTO meeting and shared my ideas for the turtles.

"I think there's a way we could have everything we want. We could still have a climbing wall, it just wouldn't stretch into the turtle area. That space would be surrounded in clear stuff, plexiglass, I think it's called, like it's a zoo. It'll have an opening toward the woods. And then we could watch the turtles come in and hatch and everything. It'll be awesome for biology lessons and will feel like the turtles are part of the playground. They'll be safe and we'll still have our wall. It won't be as long, but it'll be there."

I thanked them and returned to my seat. In the audience, four papier-mâché turtle heads nodded and cheered.

"Good job," Dad whispered.

"Thanks," I answered. "I practiced the speech with my Down with the Patriarchy club before school yesterday."

Lily twisted around in her seat in front of me. Her mom was the PTO president and she had told me earlier that she had to go to all of the meetings. "Great job," she whispered. She glanced toward where Tomkin the Human sat at the front of the room, yawning. "I wish you had won the election."

I laughed. "So you must've been the other person who voted for me."

Lily's face scrunched up. "The other person?"

I sighed. "I know I only got two votes, Lily. I heard you telling someone after the election."

Lily bit her lip. "I'm not really supposed to say this . . ." She glanced again at Tom, who had fallen asleep, then lowered her voice. "The truth is, you heard me wrong. You didn't only get two votes. You only *lost* by two votes."

❖ ❖ ❖

A week later, I wore a purple dress. Molly wore pink. I pulled her down the aisle in a little wagon and threw rose petals with my other hand. The fall air was warm on my skin. I thought I'd be sad, knowing it was the last day I'd see Grandma for a long time. But then we reached the end of the aisle and I watched Mom escort Grandma along the petal path, and there wasn't any way in the world to be sad. Not when my grandma glowed in her long tie-dyed gown like she was made out of sunshine. She had daisies pinned in her hair instead of a veil. Beside me, Mr. Bosserman wiped at a tear on his cheek with a hand-kerchief. This was a day to be happy, only happy, onest.

The aisle was really just a stretch of green grass in my backyard. On both sides were little folding chairs filled with everyone I loved on one side, and everyone Mr. Bosserman loved on the other. Sam, Sheldon, April, and Amanda and their parents sat on Mr. Bosserman's side, too.

Just as the sun was setting, the preacher announced Grandma and Mr. Bosserman wife and husband, and they kissed. And it wasn't even all that gross. Afterward, the whole backyard was turned into a dance floor. Mr. Bosserman's son, Alan Bridgeway, had asked Mom and Dad if he could contribute the decorations. Mom had thought that maybe he'd bring in some bouquets of flow-ers or an ice sculpture. He did. But he also had sent in a crew of workers who had turned our backyard into a fairyland, with strings of yellow lights swooping over-head, a little splashy fountain in the corner, and lots of little tables. Waiters and waitresses carried trays of food that looked a lot prettier than it tasted. (Have you ever had quiche? If you have, I'm sorry. If you haven't, don't.) Since it was starting to get cool at night, he even sent tall outdoor heaters.

A deejay played music, including old-timey songs by Elvis, and Grandma and Mr. Bosserman danced harder than anyone. Who knew? Mr. Bosserman, I mean, Gaga, can do a mean chicken dance. "Don't boogey too hard," Grandma told him. "We've got at least five hundred miles to drive in the morning."

But he just laughed.

Scrappy twirled April by me. He grinned and waved, his brown eyes looking even bigger behind his new glasses.

Behind them, Shemanda swayed slowly to the music, even though it was a fast song.

❖ ❖ ❖

Later, when the stars looked like more fairy lights hanging over our heads, I spotted Sam sitting alone in the last row of chairs. His cast had been off for a couple days, but he still seemed to cradle the arm against his chest when he was daydreaming.

Since Days of Yonder Faire, Sam and I had become friends again, but it wasn't quite the same as before. I didn't know if it ever would be. Both of us had said such mean things, and even though a lot of time had passed, those words were still there.

A few weeks earlier, Miss Parker had handed each person in a class a mini tube of toothpaste and a paper plate. She had asked each of us to squeeze out all the toothpaste. "Now put it back," she had said. A few of us tried, squeezing the tube or trying to push the toothpaste inside the little opening. "Hmm," she had said. "That doesn't seem to be working. Try saying sorry to the tooth-paste for squeezing it." Her face was so serious, most of us did that, too. We told the toothpaste we were sorry. "Now try to put it back."

Maybe you see where this is going. I didn't until then, though. Miss Parker continued, "Our words are like that. When we say or do something unkind, it's always going to be out there. You can say you're sorry. You can even really, truly mean it. But those words are out forever."

The mean things Sam and I had shouted to each other at the Faire would always be there. But Miss Parker had said something else, too. She said that kindness is just like that toothpaste. That every act of kindness, every time we notice someone needs us and take action, will last forever in that person's mind.

So I nabbed a slice of cake from one of the food tables and shoved it in my mouth. Then I grabbed two more and I sat down next to Sam in the shadows. "Are you having a good time?"

Sam smiled; his eyes seemed to shine a little but maybe that was the fairy lights again. He had been smiling a lot more lately. A few days after the election, Tomkin the Human had announced "his" plan for instituting clubs at school, and Sam had immediately started a running club. Every day after school, he and a bunch of other kids, including Lily, would go for long runs. Sam always led the pack. Even though our intermediate school didn't have a track team until seventh grade, when we would start middle school, I had spotted the coach watching Sam a couple of times, timer in his hand and grin on his face. Maybe running wasn't the same as gymnastics—I was sure it wasn't—but maybe it was close.

"I was just thinking about this year," Sam said with a shrug. He scooped a huge piece of cake into his mouth.

"Can you believe we're going to be in sixth grade soon?"

Sam nodded. Some of the blue icing stuck to the top of his lip. "Yeah, but that's not what I was thinking about."

"What were you thinking about?"

"Those twins. Did you know their mom and my mom have coffee a couple times a month? They're getting really big."

I put my empty cake plate down on the chair in front of me. "That's got to feel good, doesn't it? Seeing them, knowing they wouldn't be here if it weren't for you."

"It does," Sam said. He shook his head. "I don't think I really admitted that until now. I acted like it wasn't a big deal and felt so bad for myself about my arm. It was hard to take credit for something I never even had thought about. I mean, I never thought about saving the kids. I just saw the truck and the next thing I knew, I was pushing them aside. It wasn't, like, a *choice*."

"That doesn't matter. You're a hero, Sam."

"I guess so," he muttered.

I laughed. "Took you long enough to figure out!"

"That's the thing, though," Sam said. He pushed his hands through his hair and looked up at the stars. "Maybe heroes are the best when they don't even know they're heroes. Like maybe the best heroes just act." Sam pointed to where Scrappy danced with April. "Like maybe they see that a little kid isn't trying to be a brat; he just can't see. And they point it out." Sam lowered his hand and tilted his head toward Amanda, where she and Sheldon were now grabbing some punch from a fancy fountain. My mom walked by them, patting Amanda's head as she passed. "And maybe the best kind of hero realizes her friend needs a mom and shares her own. Maybe she sees that same friend make a mess and steps forward and makes it hers, too."

For some reason, I couldn't talk. I could barely breathe, even though my thought maker screamed *he's talking about us*!

"Maybe the best kind of hero knows she's probably not going to win but puts herself out there anyway." Sam pulled in a big breath. "Maybe she's even brave enough to tell her best friend when he's being a jerk and needs to stop feeling sorry for himself."

"Sam—"

"A person like that? She's a hero." He smiled, his eyes crinkling at the sides. "Just quietly heroic. In fact, maybe that's the only thing that's ever quiet about that person."

I felt my face flame and wondered if he could see the blushing in the moonlight. My eyes were watery for no reason at all. "Maybe," I whispered. "But I still think you're a better hero. I mean, a real hero."

"Just because I saved someone?" Sam laughed like it was no big deal, and scraped up another bite of cake.

"Well, yeah."

Sam's laugh turned into a cough. His hands flew up and circled his neck as he coughed more. Holy lollipop farts!

"Sam!" I yelped. "Are you choking?"

Still holding his throat, Sam nodded.

"I've got this!" I shouted and jumped to my feet. I pulled Sam upright and wrapped my arms around Sam's middle, my left hand covering my right fist under the middle of his ribs. "Get ready," I said, "I'm going Heimlich Remover you!"

Sam's choking sped up, the coughing sounds tumbling into each other so they almost sounded more like a . . .

"Are you laughing?" I dropped my arms and stomped my foot. "Samuel! Were you faking?"

Laughing so hard tears streamed down his cheeks, Sam doubled over. "It's Heimlich Maneuver, not Remover." He put his arm around my shoulder. "You're such a dork."

"A dork who would've saved your life."

Did we howl? Of course we did.

Acknowledgments

I have too many heroes to list, which is a glorious problem. But please indulge me as I name a few.

My super agent and friend Nicole Resciniti. Look how our literary pack has grown! My career wouldn't have been possible without you, and I'm so grateful.

My amazing editor, Becky Herrick. It's a privilege to work with you and the Sky Pony team, including editorial director Alison Weiss, production editor Joshua Barnaby, copy editor Denise Roeper, cover designer Brian Peterson, and Emma Dubin.

My wonderful husband, Jon. Thank you for laughing when I read excerpts aloud, for making the coffee every morning, and for allowing me to pilfer your childhood experiences for fodder. Where would this book be without an accidental goat-napping? This also seems like a good spot to publicly thank you for knowing the Heimlich Maneuver and keeping "This is the best sandwich ever" from being my last words.

My critique partners, including Lynn Rush and Emma Vrabel. Thank you for the fantastic feedback and suggestions. Thank you also to Ben Vrabel for requesting a superhero book, coming up with the title, and suggesting that Lucy could fill the role. I also appreciate the plot building you helped me develop over breakfast.

My friend Katie Miller, who offered insight into the intense world of competitive gymnastics. That being said, any errors in portraying Sam's journey are on me.

And, of course, librarians and teachers. You're my heroes.